THE CAT'S FANCY

Humans think they rule the animal kingdom, but cats know better. Every now and then, humans need a little help, and Max the Cat meets the challenge when his human Kari gets in deep doo-doo after losing her job. His solution? Kari needs a mate – and fast!

KariAnn Ingles loves her big black kitty Max, who seems to understand her so well, she suspects he can read her mind. Unfortunately, Max the Cat is very protective and runs off every date she brings home. As a result, Max is the *only* man in her life.

Max adores his human Kari. But suddenly she starts spending all day, every day, at home, not bothering to go to work. This seriously cramps his feline lifestyle, and it's time to take matters into his own paws. Kari needs a mate, and Max is on a big-kitty mission to find her the *purrr-fect* man – if there is such a creature!

Daniel Cole Jordensen is settling into his new apartment after a job transfer and breakup with his latest girlfriend. When a black cat shows up at his door and won't leave him alone, he follows him to the apartment of a charmingly unkempt young woman named Kari Ingles. Suddenly Cole's past troubles with women are eclipsed by Miss Ingles and her darned cat!

THE CAT'S FANCY

Gwen E. Ambrose

Licensed and Produced through
Penumbra Publishing
www.PenumbraPublishing.com

All rights reserved
Printed in USA
PRINT ISBN/EAN-13: 978-1-935563-03-7
Copyright 2009 Gwynn E. Ambrose

Also available EBOOK ISBN/EAN-13: 978-1-935563-13-6

~Author Foreword~

I'm an animal lover and enjoy injecting the crazy fun of animals into my stories. *The Cat's Fancy* is a light romance featuring feline exploits and how they affect humans.

While pet ownership can be a big responsibility, sharing the love of an animal has its own unique rewards. Pets can quickly endear themselves and become part of the family.

I support ethical treatment of animals. They may not always be able to speak up for themselves, but they deserve as much respect as humans!

Many of the antics described in my stories are based in part on my own interactions with animals. I'm sure pet owners everywhere will recognize similar traits and behaviors in the animals in their lives.

Animals have their own personalities and ingrained behavior patterns, and sometimes they do such a great job interacting with humans, we think they are telepathic. They may actually be – who can say for sure? It's a known fact they can sense things humans are unaware of, and in my world this ability gives them a near paranormal, magical ability well beyond the typical human.

I hope you enjoy the whimsy of animal-human interaction in this story.

In honor of some of the special animals who've been my friends or in some way touched my life, I dedicate this book to ... *Queenie, Pinky, Snowball, Lassie, Tiger, Fido, Pixie, Frisky, Jacques, Napoleon, Rusty, Daisy, Champ, Popcorn, Roscoe, Ham, Bean, Willie, Shep, Cleo, Chester, Tonka, Sassy, Morgan, Toby, Fluffster, and Shadow.*

Gwynn E. Ambrose

THE
CAT'S
FANCY

A Cat Para-Abnormal Romance

by

Gwynn E. Ambrose

CHAPTER 1

Max's World

Humans persist in the notion that they are at the top in the animal kingdom, announced Big Buddha Pest, *but we cats know better.*

As I, Max the Cat, sat in the vacant lot claimed as the usual meeting place by our loosely organized social group, I gazed at each of my comrades in the warming light of early morning. They all agreed with the assessment frequently voiced by Big Buddha Pest. His words carried weight with our group – in more ways than one. The portly, long-haired male with large orange spots on well-maintained white fur had repeated this idea often enough that it had gone unchallenged since I first attended the group. And his favorite mantra, stating cats should be 'large and in charge,' was aptly demonstrated by his girth. Big Buddha Pest was extremely well-fed.

And I would be remiss if I failed to point out, added Big Buddha Pest, *that cats are far superior in intellect and manners to the other popular human companion choice. By any scale or measure, cats are well above the dog in every way. Dogs serve their masters,* he announced with disdain, *while cats are served by their staff.*

The gray tabby tomcat known as Charlie, perched on a pile of discarded wood to my right, yawned at the worn but still appreciated sentiment. For all cats of any breeding and social standing, it was ingrained in the psyche to deplore the unfortunate lowly dog, who had to grovel for affection, beg for food, and

1

perform tricks to entertain his human masters. As a matter of instinct and personal pride, no cat would ever knowingly stoop to such demeaning behavior.

Cats rule, dogs drool, chanted the unkempt black and white spotted longhaired neutered male known as Patches. Young and easily distracted, he pounced on a stray scrap of paper that fluttered in the breeze. We all showed appropriate signs of mild amusement, hoping that in time he would mature and curtail his boisterous outbursts.

The spayed calico female named Miss Suzy-Q, lounging in the grass some distance away in our casual circle, finished licking her left paw and deigned to add, *Only by the grace of opposable thumbs do humans rule the world.*

I blinked at her with my yellow eyes, then busied myself licking a spot on my black coat ruffled by the breeze. Finished with my grooming, I looked around. No one else seemed eager to reply to Miss Suzy-Q's comment. Most of us had one or more humans dedicated to serving our wants and needs, and those who did not were polite enough not to complain. Only the snooty Miss Suzy-Q seemed haughty enough to voice that opinion aloud.

I glanced up, noting the summer morning sky becoming lighter and the air warmer. Quickly I decided to bid the group adieu and depart.

As I made my way down the alley toward my human Kari's domicile, I passed through a residential area of moderately sized older homes. The house with the faded green shutters and neglected backyard garden was the lair of an elderly human female who had kept the cat we all know as The Empress imprisoned inside her home for as long as anyone could remember.

I glanced up at the sun rising higher in the sky and chose to spare a moment to check on The Empress to see if she was about the windows of the old house. She usually resigned herself to spending a good part of each day ensconced in the bay window ledge at the front of the house.

I leapt onto the front porch railing covered with flaking, faded green paint. Casually strolling along the top rail, I glanced toward the window with its filmy pale green curtains parted to admit daylight weakened by the shadow cast from the porch.

Today The Empress appeared to be in a somewhat sedate but tolerant mood as she sat regally with her paws tucked under the great expanse of her thick, brown-tipped, buff fur. A Himalayan with the classic dark, flat face, she allowed her blue eyes to follow my movements with casual disinterest. She rarely acknowledged my presence beyond momentary eye contact, and today was no different.

I sat on the railing and gazed at her. She seemed always to be incredibly sad, and I empathized with her reluctance to show any sign of happiness after a lifetime of abuse and confinement.

She was understandably ashamed to display her paws publicly after having been 'declawed.' The removal of her appendages had forever scarred her, both physically and mentally. This I was able to glean from her pervasive aloofness and her reticence to interact with others. I had heard of this sort of thing before, and The Empress was a classic example of the terrible depression that could result from the painful injury and mutilation of having one's claws removed. I winced inwardly at the thought, but quickly recovered.

Hopping down from the railing, I hit the porch floor with barely a sound, and stretched upward on my hind legs to touch my nose to the window glass. The Empress immediately turned her head and looked away.

Unfazed, I departed and proceeded on my way home, thinking perhaps I might be cutting it a bit close to sneak back through the bent window screen and return to my human Kari's living room before she became aware of my absence.

In my infinite wisdom, I soiled the litter box a few times before leaving, to mislead Kari into believing I'd been cooped up in the apartment all night. Otherwise, she'd become suspicious over the lack of activity in the litter box, or fear I was suffering from some ailment that would prompt her to take me to the dreaded vet's office. Luckily for both of us, I thought things through thoroughly enough to avoid such needless complications. I amused myself with the irony of this situation as I trotted purposefully through the alley on my way home. I cared deeply for my human Kari, but sometimes she could be thoroughly irritating when she insisted on grabbing me up into her arms and hugging me tightly, showering me with silly nicknames like, 'my little peppercorn,' 'my little cricket,' 'Kitty-Kitty-Man,' or 'Mr. Kitty,' or 'Maxi Cat.' Especially annoying was her cooing reference to my activities in the litter box as 'a visit to Camp Kittypoopoo.'

Growling under my breath, I noted the regularity with which she verbalized the term, and fully expected her to say it again as soon as I returned home to find her scooping out the deposits I left purposely to ease her suspicions about my nightly forays.

The unexpected barking of a large dog startled me. With relief I saw he was confined in a sturdy fence. Another glance at the brightening sky urged me to hasten my trek home. My human Kari would soon depart for the place she called 'work,' leaving the apartment in quietude for my daily nap.

CHAPTER 2

Kari's Dilemma

KariAnn glanced at the clock on her nightstand, then looked around her bedroom, wondering where Max could be hiding. Knowing he'd show up when he was good and ready, she turned back to her laptop sitting on her desk and snickered as she skimmed the email joke, 'The Cat's Diary,' that Raschelle had forwarded to her. She'd seen it before, but the concept of 'day 487 of my captivity' still cracked her up. She could just imagine a cat cleverly trapping the dog in the closet and casually tripping human captors on the stairs. Whoever had authored this joke had certainly been wearing a cat-in-the-hat thinking cap.

But not all cats were devious and twisted. Her lovable Maxi Cat would never plot against her and try to deliberately trip her on the stairs in an attempt to get away from her. Max loved her, and he was way too cool and smart to do anything really mean like that. Okay, so sometimes he wove in and out between her legs, rubbing himself against her. But that was just his way of showing affection. He was her big black kitty-man. Her *only* man.

She sighed and closed her laptop as she shoved up from her desk chair. She needed to hurry and get to work on time. Thanks to Max, she was in hot water with her supervisor. *Really* hot water. Okay, it wasn't exactly Max's fault. Jeff Braswell was a jerk and deserved what happened Saturday night.

She giggled as she headed into her bathroom and turned on the shower, recalling the prelude to the incident, when Jeff had called and asked if he could come over. She thought it was weird that he'd treat her like crap at work and then think it was perfectly all right to start trying to date her when he was technically her boss. But he denied that it was a date, saying he just wanted to be 'friends,' to make up for his crabbiness at work. He made it all sound so innocent and unrehearsed. How could she not let him come over to share popcorn and watch a movie with her?

She should have known better.

It didn't take him long to ask to use the restroom, insisting he preferred the privacy of the master bathroom in her bedroom. After a few minutes, he called out to her from the bedroom. She was stunned to find he'd taken off his clothes and was waiting for her beside her bed in only his underwear and socks. While she was trying to think of a way to appropriately defuse the situation, Max took care of the problem for her – by strolling over and urinating in Jeff's shoes.

Whatever amorous plans Jeff had in mind immediately went out the window. He wasted no time vacating her apartment and tossing his soiled tennis shoes in the garbage dumpster.

Shaking her head, Kari snickered again as she peeled off her pajamas and stepped into the shower. *Good ol' Max!*

Of course now she'd have to be extra careful around Jeff. He already felt threatened by her because she'd had to train him when he was brought in as her supervisor. She still did the work he was supposed to do, while he spent most of his time surfing on the internet, only now he took credit for everything that got done in the department.

No telling what the sneak would do to get back at her after the little fiasco this weekend. She still didn't have any idea how she'd handle the awkwardness once she saw him at work. Well, maybe there wouldn't be any awkwardness. Maybe Jeff would just continue to treat her like pond scum and ignore her when he wasn't on her case about screwing up something that he'd done wrong himself.

Moments after she'd stepped out of the shower and was still drying off, she heard the phone ring. Ruffling her blonde locks with her towel, she strolled into the bedroom, wondering who'd be calling this early. As soon as she picked up the phone, she heard the velvety chocolate voice of her best friend and coworker Raschelle rasping, "Kari!"

"Raschelle, what's—"

"Lori said she saw Jeff-the-Jerk and VP Kendall walk into the HR director's office and close the door. My guess is, Jeff's trying to get you fired."

A chill riddled Kari from head to toes, and not because she wasn't wearing any clothes. "What makes you think their meeting has something to do with me?"

"Let me see ... it's before your regular shift work hours. And didn't you call me Saturday night and tell me Jeff came over and tried to get busy with you? Hello!"

Kari huffed. She'd called Chelle after Jeff left Saturday, hoping to get advice about how to handle the situation. All Chelle could do was laugh like a hyena when she told her what Max had done to Jeff's shoes, then holler about how gullible she'd been to let Jeff into her apartment in the first place. Then she reminded her that workplace romances were a bad idea on so many levels, there wasn't sufficient time to list all the reasons.

"You'd better get your white-bread butt to work right now and make like a busy little bee!" Raschelle ordered. "I heard we're getting a new district supervisor to replace Ferber, who was 'asked' to retire, and you don't want to get caught strolling in late with a new sheriff in town."

"I'm not supposed to be there for another—"

"Come in early."

"Yeah, okay, I'll be there as soon as I can."

"I'll try to find out more before you get here. Have your cell phone turned on so I can get hold of you."

"Okay, Chelle. Thanks."

"No prob, girlfriend. Gotta go. I see Jeff coming this way."

The phone went dead, and Kari hung it up, realizing this was the main reason workplace romances were never a good idea.

7

The Cat's Fancy   Gwynn E. Ambrose

Not that she would ever have considered Jeff-the-Jerk Braswell as a potential romance partner.

Consequences, consequences.

She looked around frantically. "Maxi! Where are you, my little cupcake? Mommy's gotta go to work early!"

CHAPTER 3

Cole's New Beginning

———————

Maybe it wouldn't be so bad living in Baltimore, Cole decided as he rummaged through the boxes stacked in the corner, looking for his bathroom items. As the morning sunlight peeked in from the balcony, highlighting the beige carpet underfoot, he straightened from the mess he'd made of the boxes and rubbed his stubbly chin. It wouldn't do to show up unshaven his first day as the new district office manager. Not that he was that excited about showing up at all.

Sighing, he looked around the small, drab living room of his new apartment. In the brightening light of day, it seemed smaller and more depressing than it had when he'd arrived late last night. And it would seem even smaller when the rest of the rental furniture arrived.

This is just temporary, he told himself, renewing his search for his toiletries. Until he was settled in with his new job, he didn't want to rush into buying property and moving everything he owned. Things were still up in the air – except where Beth was concerned.

It was definitely over with her. She'd said some pretty nasty things when he'd told her about his transfer. Why couldn't she understand he didn't have control over where the company sent him? If Manning Industries wanted a regional corporate office tightened up, he was their go-to man. He'd evaluate the personnel and thin the herd if necessary. It wasn't like he'd *asked* to be sent to Baltimore.

9

The Cat's Fancy

Gwynn E. Ambrose

He located a travel bag containing a razor, shaving cream, toothpaste, toothbrush, and deodorant, then headed for the bathroom.

Maybe it was for the best. The six months he'd spent with Beth had been a roller coaster ride at best ... more downs than ups. Now that he was away from her constant badgering, it was easy to admit she was vain, selfish, emotionally high-strung, and riddled with petty jealousy – too high-maintenance to make her beautiful package worth the cost. He would have found a way to break things off anyway. The job transfer just made it quicker and easier.

Sighing with relief, he patted down his slick face, then shed the tee-shirt and sweats he'd slept in. As he stepped into the shower, he tried not to think what kind of hell he'd be walking into at work. If rumors had started around the water cooler – and he was sure they had – he'd already be branded as the company hatchet man. That would only make the work he had to do more difficult. In an atmosphere of fear and distrust, he wouldn't get any straight answers from anyone. There'd be the finger-pointers who'd say anything about anybody, just to divert attention from themselves and save their own jobs. Of course there were always a few yes-man suck-ups who'd whisper unfounded gossip and skewed factoids to make it seem they were the sole saviors of the company. And the list went on.

He scrubbed his sudsy hair vigorously, trying to make that horrible list in his head go away. Working for a corporation that had grown too big for its britches definitely had its disadvantages. When he'd first started at Manning ten years ago, he'd been fresh out of college and eager to learn the ropes. Back then, the company had been Cooper & Pauley Associates, much smaller, with just one main office. He'd known the owners personally and was on good terms with them. But then they got bought out by Manning Industries.

Manning had expanded into service and software contracts in a time when that industry was in a whirlwind of technological

10

upheaval. They'd taken over smaller companies and hired too many extra people too fast to keep up with the exponentially increasing demands of the business. But as soon as the economy took a nosedive, they'd had to unload overhead expenses, and the fastest way to do that was cut personnel.

Only by the grace of being a steady producer and keeping his division productive, had Cole hung onto his managerial position. In trying to stay out of the mêlée of corporate cutthroat backbiting, he'd managed to get himself shuttled to a position that required him to go in and do 'housecleaning' in other divisions. It was not a position he enjoyed, but to remain employed, he'd had little choice. And trying to salvage what was left and make it work, he sometimes had to make unpopular and unpleasant decisions. That was exhausting and demoralizing. He no longer enjoyed his work.

Maybe it was time to look for a different kind of job, or think more seriously about going into business for himself. If only he'd done that two years ago when the economy was still booming, instead of waiting. Now it seemed he was stuck being Manning Industries' hatchet man.

Cole stepped out of the shower and dried off with a towel he pulled out of a half-unpacked box. He tried not to think of the unpleasant side of things, but right now he couldn't help it.

When his work was done here in Baltimore – the last district office Manning wanted 'streamlined' – what would become of him when there was no longer a need to swing the hatchet?

What, indeed?

CHAPTER 4

Changes in the Air

"Max! Come on! I have to go to work!"

Kari glanced nervously at the clock on her stove and dumped a pile of dry cat food into Max's ceramic bowl emblazoned with his name framed in kitty paw prints. She picked up the matching water bowl and dumped the water into the sink. Rinsing and refilling the bowl, she set it back down on the vinyl placemat on the linoleum floor and stood up. Grabbing her purse off the kitchen table, she headed for the door.

A familiar deep meow from behind her arrested her mid-step. She turned to find her large, sleek, black cat standing near his food bowl, looking up at her with his devilishly innocent yellow eyes. Instantly her nervousness abated. "There you are. Where have you been hiding?"

She dropped her purse on the floor and bent down to lift Max into her arms. He weighed nearly fifteen pounds, but there wasn't a pinch of flab on him. He was solid muscle covered in thick, velvety, midnight-black fur.

She rubbed her face over Max's silky back, and he immediately started purring loudly. "Mommy's been calling you for half an hour. Were you having a big kitty dream and couldn't wake up? Where's your secret hiding place, baby? You're going to have to be on time if you want to say good-bye to Mommy before she leaves for work."

She put him gently on the floor, and he went to his food bowl to pick out a crunchy morsel "Mommy's going to have to follow you some day and find out where you've been sleeping lately. You used to sleep all snuggled up to me, but I guess it's too hot to do that in the summertime, huh?"

She bent down and ran a hand over his luxurious coat as he nibbled on his food. "I have to go to work now. You be a good boy while I'm gone." Grinning, she grabbed her purse and headed for the door. "See you this evening, Maxi. Love ya!"

* * * * *

As soon as the door slammed shut, I stopped pretending to eat and strolled into the living room. Sitting down on the carpeted floor, I watched the door intently, waiting to see whether Kari would come back. Usually by now she would have discovered something she forgot, and be fiddling with her key to get the door open. But I heard nothing, so I felt certain she was gone for the duration of the day.

I stretched leisurely, trying to work out the kinks of stress in my back and shoulders. Rushing back to the apartment just in time to find Kari yelling for me had made me somewhat nervous, and it was difficult for me to purr contentedly when she grabbed me up for a hug.

Usually she didn't leave for work quite this early, so something must have happened to disturb her routine. Whatever it was hadn't seemed to cause any problems. My litter box was clean, my food bowl was full of my favorite dry cat food she oftentimes complained was the most expensive, and I had fresh water. She'd even left a saucer of milk, a saucer of my delicious gravy-laden 'wet' food, and had scattered some special treats in the floor nearby. A few dirty dishes leftover from her meal last night still sat in the sink. Everything seemed normal.

Yawning, I dismissed my nagging worry and strolled toward the bedroom. My normal routine involved snoozing during the hottest part of the day, and then venturing out at in the evening while Kari watched TV, or later at night after she'd gone to bed and was fast asleep. My nighttime forays often involved chasing the occasional rodent through the bushes and looking into other apartments lit up in the darkness. I particularly enjoyed the activity resulting when a dog inside sensed my presence outside and went wild with a fit of barking, soon to be followed by a fit of human yelling that usually included the words, 'Shut up!' I purred at the thought and hopped up on Kari's rumpled bed.

Pushing around with my front paws, I kneaded a section of bed clothing relatively undisturbed by Kari's sleep movements. Despite the slight upset to my normal routine caused by Kari's early departure, I saw no reason to suspect this day would go any differently from the rest. Settling down, I closed my eyes to the daylight dimmed by the curtains covering the window. Immediately I drifted off in soft slumber.

* * * * *

As Kari breezed into the cubicle she shared with Raschelle, her best friend shot her a shifty-eyed look that skewed toward the far end of the open warehouse-style cubicle farm. Before Kari could explain about the wreck on Interstate 95 that caused her to arrive ten minutes late, Raschelle touched her elegantly long cinnamon-colored fingers to her earphone and smiled her famous neon-toothy grin. "Of course, Mr. Sandusky, feel free to call back anytime. I'm always glad to be of help."

With a huff, Kari stuffed her purse into her desk drawer, then slid into her chair. Fiddling with her earphone, she turned on her computer and looked at the large clock mounted on the wall ahead. At least Jeff Braswell wasn't leaning over her cubicle wall to point out her tardiness. So much for small favors.

She turned around to see if Raschelle was finished with her help-desk call. She and Chelle were charged with handling the medical software calls, and their days varied from dead to frantic, depending on what time of day or day of the week it happened to be. Fridays afternoons were always the worst, despite the fact that more people took off on Fridays than all other days combined. Thank goodness it was Monday.

Chelle sat regal and tall in her chair, with her long, wavy, copper tresses perfectly coiffed and betraying the glistening stiffness of straightened, permed, and colored African-American hair. She tapped her earphone again to end the call, then turned to contemplate Kari. "I thought you were coming in *early*."

Kari glanced around cautiously. Half the cubicles in the expansive room had been empty for months, and there was talk of even more layoffs. She might have had a better chance of advancement if the service center manager hadn't known Jeff Braswell personally and hired him for the job of call center supervisor as a personal favor. Raschelle filled an ethnic quota, so she seemed safe for the time being. Kari got the awful task of bringing Jeff up to speed to be their incompetent, uncaring boss. Now the need for that tutoring seemed close to an end.

"So," Kari whispered, "did you hear anything else about the closed-door meeting?"

Raschelle shook her head. She started to say something, but her line buzzed, and she got another call. A second later, Kari's line buzzed, and she immediately got sucked into a call of her own. Minutes passed that seemed like hours as Kari sifted through arcane information on her computer to answer oddball questions for a remote user trying to do something with the software it wasn't designed to do. As she ended the call, she looked up to find Jeff Braswell scowling down at her over the cubicle wall.

"You need to come to HR," he growled. "Now."

Kari turned and rose to her feet, catching Raschelle shooting Jeff a dagger glare while she talked all sweetness and light to a user on the line. Kari finger-waved, then skirted around her desk.

"Get your purse and whatever other junk you dragged in with you," Jeff ordered.

Kari felt her stomach plummet as she stopped and turned to

get her purse out of her desk drawer. Raschelle started to pull her earphone off, but Kari put a hand up and mouthed, "It's okay."

Kari knew it wasn't okay, but she didn't want Raschelle getting in hot water over something she couldn't do anything about.

Following Jeff down the long corridor between the rows of empty cubicles, Kari resisted the urge to look back over her shoulder, suspecting this would be the last time she'd ever lay eyes on the place.

* * * * *

The sound of the door slamming woke me with a start. I perked up on the bed and heard someone in the kitchen, tossing things around. Frozen in place, I waited to hear the familiar sound of my human Kari's voice, but instead heard strange gurgling noises. Realizing it was still morning, I silently jumped to the floor, wondering why someone would be in the apartment at this early hour. I padded toward the kitchen, sneaking forward to spy on what was going on and who was responsible for it.

I was surprised to see Kari's back as she stood in front of the sink. She seemed to be quaking with what I could only guess was laughter. But when she turned around and revealed her wet, ravaged face, I knew something was terribly wrong. I meowed, curious and alarmed.

"Come here, baby kitty, and give Mommy a hug." She reached for me, but I was so disturbed by this sudden turn of events, I wanted to flee until I better understood the situation. Moving too late, I found myself scooped up in Kari's arms while she buried her face in my fur and murmured, "It'll be okay, baby. Everything will be okay."

Her words worried me, and I struggled to get down. She set me on the floor and reluctantly let me go, stroking my back as I scurried to the far side of the kitchen and watched her, wide-eyed. What had happened to upset her so? Until I knew, I'd remain upset too.

Kari grabbed a napkin from the kitchen table, blew her nose, and tossed the napkin in the trash can. Sighing forlornly, she trudged toward the bedroom. I followed cautiously, worried about how this would affect things. Clearly her behavior – coming home so soon after leaving for work – was an unexpected change in her routine, and she didn't seem happy about it. I could only hope that things would return to normal soon ... very soon.

* * * * *

Cole arrived at Manning's Baltimore office at 10:05. He decided to let everyone settle into their normal routine before showing up to destroy it.

Announcing himself to the receptionist, he asked to see the director of Human Resources, then waited. The receptionist, a round-cheeked little gal who appeared to be in her forties, kept looking at him like she thought he was going to pull a gun or sprout a second head. He smiled and ignored her, checking his watch to see how long it would take Gerald Vance to work up the nerve to meet with him.

Surprisingly, Vance only took ten minutes. Maybe he was a direct man who liked to get unpleasant confrontations out of the way quickly. But Cole doubted it. He gave the receptionist a warm smile as she directed him to Vance's office.

"Welcome to Baltimore, Mr. Jordensen," Vance said, meeting him at the door of his glass-front office. He ushered him in rather than remain seated at his desk to foolishly try and establish territorial dominance. At this point, everybody knew the game was over.

Cole shook hands briefly with Vance and made a quick visual assessment of him. In his fifties, with thinning hair and a gaunt face, the man dressed well and apparently kept himself fit. He was well paid to sit on his little mountaintop, but he didn't carry much responsibility when it came to running the business.

He handled personnel issues.

Cole sat down facing Vance as the man took his seat behind the desk. Allowing him a moment to get settled, Cole cleared his throat and then said, "I trust Art Billings in Houston explained the situation."

Vance nodded. "You'll be looking over personnel files and assessing the productivity of our various operations here. I've been told to give you full cooperation. Our management team has been briefed and is fully on board. Whatever you need, just ask."

"I appreciate that," Cole said. What he didn't bother to point out was that the management team might be on board now, until it came to protecting their own jobs.

"Before I meet personally with everyone," Cole continued, "I'd like to go over the files with you and review any recent personnel reductions."

"Of course," Vance said amiably. "I'm sure you'll be pleased to know that I've already taken steps to cull potential troublemakers and problematic workers from the staff."

Cole frowned. In his experience, those branded as 'troublemakers' by management were usually the ones who told the truth about how terrible things were within the company. "I prefer that no one try to do my job for me before I get here to do it."

About to hand Cole a file, Vance withdraw cautiously and cleared his throat. "Of course, Mr. Jordensen. I wouldn't presume to usurp your authority in such matters."

Cole smirked. "I'm sure you wouldn't." He leaned forward and snatched the file from Vance's limp hand. Sitting back, he opened the file and skimmed it quickly. "And what did Miss Ingles do to raise your ire, prompting you to fire her this morning, just before I arrived?"

Vance covered his mouth and coughed discreetly. "There was a potential sexual-harassment issue I felt should be dealt with before it became problematic."

Cole raised his brows in amazement. Perhaps things were

worse here than he'd been led to believe...

* * * * *

"So, how are you doing?" Raschelle asked in her dusky phone-sex voice that made her so popular with the users of call-support. She forced an arm around Kari's shoulders as she pushed into the apartment, past the door Kari held onto as a barrier.

"I'm okay," Kari grumbled, trying to be gracious, but failing miserably. "Really, Chelle, you didn't have to come over. I'm not exactly in the mood for company."

"Honey, I'm not company, I'm your friend." Chelle glanced around the living room as she sat down on the red upholstered couch. "Where's that devil-cat of yours?"

"Don't worry. Max is off doing his own thing." Kari sighed and slumped down in one of the two black and white op-art chairs arranged opposite the red couch. She wiped her face, embarrassed that she'd lain around and moped all day, sleeping most of the time when she could have been straightening the place up – or filing for unemployment compensation online. She'd left the apartment in a mess when she'd gone to work this morning. When she'd returned a couple hours later, she was in no mood to clean house or deal with her sudden lack of income.

Anyway, so what if she'd left some mail on the coffee table, and stuff was a little dusty? Chelle had seen it in worse shape, and she wasn't a white-glove inspector. She had her own place too, and she knew what it took to keep things up. Of course Chelle probably had somebody come in and clean her townhouse once a week. It was always spotless and perfect whenever Kari went over there.

"I can't believe they escorted you out of the building and didn't even let you get your stuff from your desk!" Chelle's golden eyes flickered with anger as she plopped a small cardboard box onto the coffee table. "When you didn't come back, I figured what happened and gathered it up for you."

The Cat's Fancy

Gwynn E. Ambrose

"Thanks," Kari ground out as new tears threatened to flood her eyes. She swiped at them and reached for the five-by-seven framed picture of Max sticking up out of the box. He was sitting on the edge her bed, looking all proud and pretty, as usual. Eyeing the picture brought a grin that quickly crumbled into a grimace, giving way to one sob and then another.

"Oh, honey, it'll be okay," Chelle said, moving around the coffee table to give her a comforting pat on the back. "You're smart and pretty, and you'll find another job in no time. And meanwhile," she added conspiratorially, "you'll be filing a sexual harassment suit against Jeff Braswell and Manning Industries."

"What?" Kari rose up from her chair and wiped her face. "Are you crazy? I need my unemployment benefits. I don't want to do anything to jeopardize that."

"You can't let them get away with this crap, Kari! Look at the facts. Braswell gets hired as *our boss* through nepotism. *You* get the job of showing him the ropes, and he treats you like dirt and disrespects you when the job should have been yours to begin with. Then he comes over here, into your *home*, and tries to get friendly with you. And two days later, he gets you fired?" She shook her index finger back and forth. "Uh-uh. That don't fly."

Kari frowned, turning slowly to face Raschelle. "You think he got me fired on purpose because ... because he was afraid I'd say something about what he tried here Saturday?" She shook her head. "But he said he just wanted to be friends."

"Oh, honey ... wake up and smell the testosterone!" Chelle put her hands on her hips and tossed her head back with a snort. "Jeff Braswell doesn't have a clue how to be anyone's friend. He's just a creepy little horndog. Anyway, what kind of friend sneaks into your bedroom and takes his pants off without even bothering to ask if you're game for it?" She snorted again. "He's a nut job, and he had no business coming over here in the first place. He was just trying to use you, and when you didn't play along, he threw the first punch by firing you to protect himself and his own job."

Kari held up her hands. "What could he possibly have said to get me fired? I didn't do anything wrong."

Raschelle shook her head, a worried look crossing her face. "I don't know, but I'll do my best to find out. Meanwhile, you file for unemployment so you can stay afloat until we figure out what to do. As soon as I know what we're up against, we'll look at our options." Her face lit up as she remembered something. "Oh, by the way, some new guy showed up after you left."

"New guy?"

"Daniel Jordensen. Lori was working the reception desk and said he was *gorgeous*. I didn't see him. But apparently he's going to be interviewing everyone."

Kari slumped back in her chair. "He must be the hatchet man everyone's been talking about."

"Yeah. Probably. Lori said he went straight to Vance's office."

Kari looked up at Chelle. "What about *your* job?"

Chelle shrugged nonchalantly. "Hey, I'm the only one left in the medical software section of the call center now. Who needs a supervisor if there's hardly anyone to supervise? My bet is, Jeff-the-Jerk will be next on the chopping block. He screwed up getting rid of you."

Kari buried her face in her hands and shook her head. Chelle bent down and gave her another hug. "Hang in there, girlfriend. Mama's not gonna let nothin' bad happen. If anything, I'll talk to Hatchet Man myself and get your job back."

Kari felt tears of relief and gratitude flood her eyes as she stood up and hugged Chelle. "Thanks. I don't know what I'd do without you."

"I'll tell you what you *are* gonna do. You're gonna kick some Braswell butt!"

Kari pulled back. "Chelle, don't do anything stupid and get yourself in trouble over this. It's not worth your job too."

"Honey, don't you worry. Mama's got it under control." She looked back behind Kari as she warned, "You just keep that darn black cat of yours under control. He's a menace to society, snagging clothes and such."

Kari managed a smile. "If it weren't for Max, I probably would have had a harder time getting rid of Jeff Saturday night. Max took care of him right away, and in seconds he was gone."

Chelle harrumphed, then nodded in agreement. "Guess you're right. That little devil doesn't waste any time running off somebody he doesn't like."

"But he really does like *you*, Chelle," Kari added quickly.

"Yeah. He likes my clothes to sharpen his claws on."

Kari still felt bad about the silk pants Chelle had to discard after Max uncharacteristically skewered her legs while she sat on the couch. Kari had insisted on paying for the pants, but Chelle refused, promising she'd wear jeans the next time she came over.

"I'll call you when I find out something more about things at work," Chelle said. "Let me know if you need anything. I'm here for you, girlfriend."

CHAPTER 5

Adjustments

———————————

When I returned to the apartment from my early-morning foray, I made sure to get back in plenty of time before Kari would leave for work. As expected, she was still sleeping when I went into the bedroom to check on her.

I groomed myself thoroughly, then strolled through the living room, looking for anything that might amuse me until Kari awoke. But nothing struck my fancy, so I returned to the bedroom. The light streaming in between the blind slats told me it was past time for Kari to get up and get ready for work.

Perhaps she had forgotten again to set that dreaded alarm on her bedside clock. I thoroughly despised the intense and irritating sound it made, and usually managed to wake her just before it went off. Still, most of the time she forgot to turn it off, and it would blare through the bedroom the whole time she was in the shower.

At the mere thought of that, I jumped up on the bed, intent on getting her awake and ready for work...

* * * * *

Kari awoke with a start as Max jumped on the foot of the bed. Bits of bright morning light streamed in between the slats in the window blinds, alerting her to the fact that she'd overslept. She reached for the bedside alarm, trying to figure out why it had not gone off to wake her at her usual time. Just as she saw the alarm wasn't set, she remembered. *No work today. No more job.*

The realization stung her, and she flopped back down in the bed, instantly as depressed as she'd been last night when she'd finally fallen asleep. Because of Jeff Braswell... She screwed up her face in a fierce frown. *Why let that butt-head continue to ruin my life? I'm free of him now.*

A smile spread across her mouth as she lay staring up at the ceiling. She rubbed her eyes and stretched. She would deliberately revel in the fact that she could wake up at her leisure without the blaring of a stupid alarm ordering her to face another day of insults and dirty looks from a man – no, a jerk pretending to be a man – whose sole purpose in life had been to make her miserable.

Yesterday, after Chelle left, she'd finally worked up the gumption to file for her unemployment online. After surmounting that hurdle, the rest of the evening hadn't seemed so bad.

Now she could look forward to a new day without worrying about any backlash from Jeff Braswell. She hadn't realized how terrible her dread of going to work had become – all because of that horse's rear she'd had to smile and be nice to while she trained him to be her boss. She scowled. Nobody ever said life was fair.

A familiar rumbling meow brought her back to reality. She sat up and smiled, facing the huge yellow eyes staring at her from a canvas of black fur silhouetted at the foot of her bed. "Morning, kitty baby. Is Mommy's boy ready for breakfast?"

With another meow that sounded a bit disgruntled, Max jumped off the bed and disappeared from sight. Kari stretched again, then climbed out of bed, feeling suddenly like a huge weight had been lifted from her shoulders. For the first time in months, she thought about venturing into the spare bedroom where she kept her drawing table and painting supplies. Maybe today would be a good day to straighten things up in there – perhaps even start a new painting. She actually felt creative, a rare feeling in the last six months since Jeff Braswell had clouded her life.

She darted into the bathroom to take care of business, then headed for the kitchen to see about Max's needs. The sun streamed into the kitchenette, making her mood even cheerier. *Yes, today would be a good day to start something new.*

* * * * *

With intense eagerness, I followed Kari into the Closed Door Room, the only room I'd been denied entry.

The Closed Door has never stopped me from testing its solidness with the weight of my body pressed against it, nor has it kept me from trying to twist the doorknob with my paws – a feat that has, once or twice, gained me entry into the bathroom or other rooms Kari, on a whim, decided she didn't want me to enter.

Of course, once I got inside past the Closed Door, the lure of the unknown instantly vanished. I was still curious about the room's contents, but the room itself appeared to be unspectacular, so I concentrated on looking around to carefully choose my first focus of investigation. I glanced at Kari and found she seemed equally interested in the contents of the Closed Door room.

The enticement of strange odors not found anywhere else in the apartment drew me upward to investigate, but the footing was precarious, at best...

"Maxi, honey, stay off those shelves. Get down! Come on, hurry up, before they topple over on you."

As Kari charged purposefully toward me, I leapt off my perch, causing the flimsy metal shelves to shake and shimmy. Kari placed a hand against the top shelf to steady the whole affair back against the wall as I shook myself off and strolled away to investigate a box sitting under a table.

"Stay out of that, Max. I know you're curious, but I don't want you getting paint on your nose. No telling what shape all this stuff is in. It's going to take me hours to sort through it all."

The Cat's Fancy

Gwynn E. Ambrose

I shook off Kari's warning and ambled away, pretending disinterest in the box I would soon return to for a more thorough inspection once she wasn't looking. A collection of long sticks caught my eye, and I jumped up on a side table to sniff them out. They might be good for chewing. I often find that chewing on small twigs is a good way to clean my teeth.

"Maxi, don't chew on Mommy's paint brushes, honey. They're coated with a protective layer of varnish, and they have old paint stuck to them."

About to take one of the sticks and make off with it in my mouth, I meowed my displeasure at Kari's continual complaining and hopped down from the small table. Off to find something else of interest, I turned to see her settling into a chair, as if she planned to spend dedicated time in here. The thought struck me that she was not preparing herself to go to work today, and she had just spent the previous two days not going to work. I recognized that pattern that she called 'the weekend' and knew that once it was over, she should be returning to work as usual. Why wasn't she going to work? This couldn't be good, not good at all...

"Maxi, honey, why are you staring at me like that?" Kari ran her fingers through her rumpled hair. "Yeah, you're right. I should get cleaned up before I let myself get distracted by all this mess. Come on, baby. I've apparently got plenty of time on my hands now to take care of setting things up again to paint."

She coaxed me out of the Closed Door Room and closed the door just as my tail cleared the doorway. I meowed loudly, wondering what this change in routine could mean. I was certain now that it could mean nothing good for me. I was a creature of habit, and any change was always disturbing.

CHAPTER 6

Lies and Other Stories

Sitting behind the desk of an office recently vacated by another seemingly useless vice-president at Manning Industries' Baltimore office, Cole scowled at Jeff Braswell's whistle-clean personnel file. He reviewed his hiring record as the small-framed fellow sat in nervous silence.

"So," Cole prodded, looking up to face Jeff Braswell, "you were hired as the call-center supervisor six months ago to replace Amanda Hemming, who retired?"

Jeff leaned forward slightly. "Yes, sir."

Cole looked back down at Jeff's file and flipped through it, not finding what he was looking for. "I don't see any prior experience in the software or customer service area that would indicate your qualifications for a supervisory position." He closed the file. "You have an uncle who works in the IT department?"

Jeff nodded his head as Cole faced him again. Cole frowned and leaned back in his chair. Clicking a pen repeatedly, he glanced aside and paused for a moment to let Jeff squirm. Sitting forward, he propped his elbows on the desk. "And your uncle is good friends with HR VP Vance."

Jeff's mouth fell open. After a second, he murmured, "Yes, sir."

With that information established, Cole decided to take another tack. "And the most senior member of the call center, KariAnn Ingles, was charged with the task of training you to become familiar enough with the department's operation so that you could assume the position of supervisor?"

Jeff squirmed in his chair. "Well, sir, I wouldn't exactly say that she *trained* me."

"What would you say she did?"

"Um ... actually, she was really hard to work with. She was resentful and disrespectful, and created a lot of problems to deliberately sabotage me, trying to make me look incompetent."

"Really." Cole leaned back in his chair again and stared hard at Jeff. "That's not exactly the way Mary Trimbull described the situation."

Jeff's mouth opened and closed several times before he was able to squeak out, "You actually spoke with Trimbull? She was let go two months ago."

"For being a 'troublemaker.'" Cole tapped another file sitting in front of him.

"Yes, everyone in the call center resented the fact that I was hired in as their supervisor. They all tried to give me a hard time."

"I see." Cole clicked his pen again. "Perhaps it was your lack of experience and your inability to properly lead the department that was the cause of everyone's resentment."

Jeff opened his mouth again, but wisely said nothing. After another pause to let Jeff think about that, Cole brought up the real issue at the heart of this interview. "Tell me about the potential sexual harassment incident that prompted you to advise HR VP Vance to let Miss Ingles go last week."

Jeff looked like a fish out of water, gasping helplessly on the bank. He swallowed several times and rubbed his chin that didn't seem capable of producing anything thicker than peach fuzz. "Um ... well ... it's actually a bit embarrassing to talk about."

"We're both adults, hopefully professional enough to ignore personal embarrassment to discuss an issue that could negatively impact this company. Enlighten me."

"Well..." He paused as if to get his story straight, obviously surprised by Cole's directness. "She ... um ... kind of ... kept trying to come on to me."

"How?"

Jeff shrugged. "Well ... she kept asking if I wanted to go out with her. I told her that was inappropriate, because technically I was her supervisor, but she didn't want to listen. The situation made me very uncomfortable."

Cole sat there, looking at Jeff Braswell, wondering what kind of woman would be desperate enough to hit on somebody like him. Before he could come to terms with the idea, Braswell added, "She just wouldn't let up. I reported the situation to VP Vance, and he decided that before things got out of hand, it would be best to let her go."

Cole nodded once. "Thank you for explaining the situation, Mr. Braswell. I'll be checking with you again, once I've had an opportunity to investigate this further."

"Of course, sir." Jeff Braswell rose from his chair and leaned forward to shake hands with Cole, but Cole deftly turned aside, pretending not to see the gesture. Jeff quickly retracted his hand and left. Cole grabbed the next file in his stack, on one Raschelle LaVonne Devreaux.

* * * * *

Raschelle breezed into Daniel Jordensen's office, feeling no fear. She was ready to have it out with the handsome, dark-haired Hatchet Man.

"Miss Devreaux." Jordensen greeted.

Before he could say anything else, Chelle propped her hands on her hips and blurted, "I know you've already talked to Jeff Braswell, and I'm pretty sure he's told you a pack of lies, but I'm here to tell you that jerk is a sneaky snake, and if you believe a thing he says, you're as big a jerk as he is!"

Jordensen blinked his big brown eyes and quickly stood up. "Have a seat, Miss Devreaux. I'm interested in hearing what you have to say."

The Cat's Fancy Gwynn E. Ambrose

"Oh, really. I just bet you are." She pointed her flame-orange fingertip at him and warned, "I was looking for a job when I cam here, and I'll be looking for another one when I wipe my feet of this place. So if you're gonna do like the rest of this yellow-bellied management bunch and fire anybody that doesn't say, 'Yes, sir,' then you can kiss my–"

"Please," Jordensen said. "Have a seat and calm down. I'm interested in learning the truth, and I'm eager to listen to what you have to say."

She harrumphed and plopped down in the armchair in front of his desk. "Fine. But I'm warning you, you're not gonna like what I'm gonna tell you. It ain't pretty."

He almost smiled as he said, "On the contrary, I think I'll be very pleased to hear what you have to say."

She narrowed her eyes suspiciously. Either this guy was clueless, or he was a really slick operator. She'd find out soon enough.

* * * * *

When Raschelle Devreaux left his office, Cole was sure of two things: she was good friends with recently terminated Kari Ingles, and the story she told about Jeff Braswell going to Kari's house was totally opposite the story Jeff Braswell told about Miss Ingles trying to hit on him. Somebody was lying, and after talking with other former employees – those who would even agree to answer his questions – he had a pretty good idea who was telling the truth and who was not. The point had come that he was ready to contact Miss Ingles and get her side of the story – if she'd talk to him.

CHAPTER 6

Curiosity

———————————

After several days, Kari had become engrossed in spending much time in the Closed Door Room. She often closed the door to keep me out, but after smelling the odd scents coming from under the door and seeing her hands splattered with unsightly spots, I decided that she could keep the Closed Door Room to herself.

This gave me plenty of opportunity to venture out of the apartment at my leisure, even during the day, without worrying that she would miss me enough to begin a search in earnest to find me and chance discovering me secret point of exit and entry. I felt a new sense of freedom, and fully intended to explore it. However that excitement was quickly dampened by worry.

Kari had talked with her friend Chelle, who liked to wear clothing of enticing smooth fabric that made me want to caress and pick it with my claws. But I had quickly learned that was not acceptable behavior, and so I kept my distance from Chelle. In overhearing Kari's conversations with Chelle, I learned just enough to realize that something apparently very important – something called *money* – would be in short supply, due to someone denying Kari a claim to it.

I didn't understand how this might impact me until Kari suddenly stopped feeding me my favorite gravy-laden food from the little cans that had dwindled and disappeared from the cabinet where she normally kept them stored. I used my paws to open the cabinet and searched the area thoroughly, but found to my dismay that the cans were indeed gone. And according to Kari's tearful apology, there would be no more forthcoming anytime soon. Luckily I did have dry cat food to sustain me, but that was really no consolation.

In a late-afternoon foray to distract my worries, I prowled the upper balconies to look in the sliding glass doors of other apartments. But many of the curtains were drawn, and I found little to occupy my thoughts as I wondered how I could possibly assist Kari in obtaining the all-important item known as *money*. I wanted my little cans of gravy-laden goodies, and it was now obvious to me that this mysterious *money* was critical to Kari's continued ability to provide for my needs. Her well-being, and mine, apparently depended solely on her continued access to *money* – which was now being hampered by her not going to the place she called 'work.'

Saddened by my inability to come up with an appropriate solution, I found myself at the glass doors of an apartment that had been, the last time I checked, unoccupied. That no longer seemed to be the case.

I paced back and forth in front of the glass doors, noting they were slightly parted. Beyond, I could see furniture and a few boxes sitting around. Some human had moved in, and I was mildly curious to find out more about the situation. As I stood peering into the living area, the entrance door to the apartment opened, and a tall human male stepped in. He was dressed in clothing that matched smartly in color and texture. He looked very neat and well-groomed. I immediately took more interest in him.

He removed the top portion of his outfit to reveal a white shirt. With his human paws, he jerked at the thin colored strip of fabric surrounding his neck like a dreaded collar. I, of course, refuse to wear one, despite my human Kari's many attempts to put one on me, and so I understood and sympathized with this human's eagerness to remove his collar. He pulled it loose and threw it aside on his couch as he plopped down and collapsed. He looked tired or upset.

Mildly curious as to why the man was out of sorts, I stared through the balcony doors. The man took a deep breath, then hoisted himself up from the couch, taking his top outer garment and neck collar with him. He disappeared past the glass doors, instantly increasing my curiosity.

I pawed at the doors, discovering that they were quite heavy, like those in my human Kari's apartment. But since they were already parted, it was easier for me to budge them slightly with my body and wedge myself inside. I looked cautiously around the main living area and noted noise coming from the area I guessed was the bedroom, laid out similarly to the apartment where Kari and I lived. Assuming the man was busy changing clothes, because that was what Kari did – or used to do – as soon as she returned home from the place she called work, I allowed myself a quick glance around.

Afternoon light came in through the open drapes, lighting the area with a warm glow. The main living area was vaguely similar to Kari's abode, but quite different in important ways. With the furniture a different color and texture, all bland solids, this room had quite a different look from my usual surroundings. Kari preferred bright and bold designs. This blandness I found somehow comforting, and immediately I felt at ease, even though I had to remind myself that I had entered a stranger's living area – a stranger whose inclinations I knew nothing about.

I looked aside and listened for telltale noises that would indicate the stranger was returning to the main living area. Satisfied that he would be occupied in his sleeping area for a while, I strolled forward to investigate the couch and matching chair that looked huge and comfy compared to the spare lines of Kari's furniture. I rubbed my face against the edge of the couch, finding the fabric soft and inviting.

The idea of snuggling into the huge folds of the couch irresistibly appealed to me, and before I knew it, I had gauged the distance and made the leap. As I pushed my paws repeatedly and deeply into the giving cushion, I found my estimation of the couch's comfort could not compare to its true luxuriousness. The urge to curl up on the couch overwhelmed me – until a sound startled me back to reality.

I looked over to find the man standing near the entrance to the short hallway that led to the bedrooms and bathrooms beyond. Dressed in jeans and a shirt with the sleeves rolled up, he wore a surprised look on his face. "How did *you* get in here?" he asked in a warm, deep voice that I found somehow reassuring, despite my natural tendency to fear anything I wasn't thoroughly sure was safe.

We looked at each other for a moment – he standing still at the far end of the room, and me standing frozen in place on his couch. He didn't make any attempt to scare or shoo me away, but I remained tense, ready to leap for the balcony doors at the first sign of trouble.

"I have to confess, I've never been much of a cat person," he said calmly, staring at me as if trying to anticipate my next move.

I turned around and jumped off his couch, quickly getting my bearings to estimate the speed and distance required to reach my only exit safely. I watched him warily as I took a tentative step, and then another, toward his sliding glass doors. Still, he didn't make any move to try to block or apprehend me.

"You're a handsome black devil, aren't you?" he commented as I strolled cautiously toward the glass doors. "Well fed. Well groomed. Obviously someone has been taking good care of you." Eyeing the parted doors as I approached them, he said, "Ah, so that's how you found your way in here."

Constantly keeping watch on him, I reached the glass doors and turned to make sure he was not going to pursue me. He stood perfectly still. We stared at each other for a moment, and in that instant I could sense he was a safe human who would not harm me.

I meowed and then turned toward the parting of the glass doors, quickly slithering outside to his balcony. I looked back to find he had moved closer to the doors to see me. We stared again at each other, and then he laughed softly, saying, "Drop in again anytime, buddy. We'll slug back a couple milks."

He moved away from the doors toward the kitchen area. I peered from a safe distance into the unoccupied living room for several more seconds before deciding I should go check on Kari. Leaping to the next balcony, I made my way home.

CHAPTER 7

Intervention

_____

By the time I made my way across several balconies and slipped in through the bent screen of the small living room window Kari kept hidden behind heavy curtains, I heard her raised voice speaking to someone. She had left the window cracked early in the spring, and had – luckily for me – forgotten she had done so. I'd been coming and going through that window and squeezing through the bent screen for some time without raising her suspicions. Now I slithered past the drapes and cautiously peeked toward the sound of Kari's elevated voice. I could tell she was upset...

"No, Mom, everything's fine. I told you, there's just a small delay in getting my first unemployment check. Yes, I have some money in my savings account. Yes, it's enough to last a while."

I approached the kitchen with care and found Kari dressed in tennis shoes, wrinkled gray sweats pants, and a tee-shirt spotted with odd colors, some of which I had trouble identifying, as my feline range of color recognition is apparently somewhat narrower than that of the common human. In any case, I recognized a slight odd scent to her clothes that was peculiar to the Closed Door Room, and new that Kari hand been doing something in there she called 'painting.' While she was doing this painting, she kept the Closed Door Room closed, insisting I occupy myself in a different part of the apartment. Most of the time I chose to entertain myself by roaming outside. She was so busy painting with the door closed, she obviously had no idea I ventured outdoors in the light of day, in addition to my frequent nightly forays.

Now, looking at her wiping her eyes and trying to keep her voice even as she spoke to the object she held in her hand and referred to as the 'phone,' I wanted to turn right around and disappear again. However, her dire emotional state intrigued me to the point that I decided I should find out what was causing her to suffer this distress. I sat down in the doorway to the kitchen and watched her as she continued talking.

"I don't know the exact amount, Mom. I don't have a bank statement in front of me. Yes, I'm sure it's enough. For at least two months. Yes." She ran her fingers through her disheveled hair. "No, I don't want you and Dad sending me any money. You can't afford that, not with Dad's unemployment about to run out. The economy's not as bad here. I'll find another job soon. Yeah, I'm sure. Don't worry. Please."

Kari turned and saw me sitting and watching her. She immediately returned her attention back to the phone. "I gotta go, Mom. I have a lot of stuff to do. Yeah, updating my résumé. Love you. Tell Dad I love him too, and not to give up. I'm sure he'll find another job sometime soon." She turned her head away from the phone and took a deep breath, then spoke into it again. "I wish there was something more I could do to help you guys out." She wiped her eyes again. "Yeah, okay, love you too. Bye."

I meowed as Kari placed the phone on its perch sitting on the counter. She came over to me and grabbed me up into her arms. "It'll be okay, baby. Mommy's going to figure something out. That mean ol' Manning Industries isn't going to send us to the poor house if I can help it."

I wiggled in her arms, and she set me down, focusing on the phone again. As she reached for it, I realized she was probably going to talk to it again for a long time, and so I headed for the living room, continually looking over my shoulder to make sure she didn't see me climbing out the window again.

The Cat's Fancy

Gwynn E. Ambrose

* * * * *

Unsettled by my human Kari's emotional distress, and not really understanding the cause of it – except that it involved that all-important item, *money* – I leapt from balcony to balcony. When I stopped, I found myself standing in the approaching twilight of early evening, staring through the same balcony that had allowed me entry into the apartment of the man who'd recently begun occupying the abode inside. The doors were now closed, and the hanging strips of fabric apparently designed to cover the doors and keep outsiders from seeing in, were now pulled shut.

I paced back and forth at the closed glass doors, pondering why I had returned here. The man had not invited me in, nor had he tried to coax me toward him when he discovered me investigating his couch earlier. Was it the couch that drew me back with its promise of soft and cushy comfort? Or was it the feeling of quiet security I had felt when staring into the human man's eyes? He was neither threatening nor encouraging, but seemed content to allow me to make my own choices in his presence. I was ... curious. I wanted to investigate him more thoroughly.

I sat down facing the closed and curtained glass doors, thinking back on how my human Kari had shown interest in a few human males. Sure she been searching for a mate, I was convinced by her poor choices that she was incapable of selecting an appropriate match. All the men she'd brought home with her were clearly wrong for her, and I'd had to sometimes go to great lengths to convince her of that. But this man ... this man who'd recently moved in, seemed kind and strong and calm – all good traits that would work to balance Kari, especially now that she was no longer going to that place she called work to get the all-important thing called money.

She had clearly lost her focus and purpose, and now

seemed determined to spend an inordinate amount of time in the Closed Door Room. Although she appeared content doing so, she still seemed distressed, and her holing up in the Closed Door Room for hours at a time left me on my own in a way that was not consistent with the routine I had come to know and expect. I found this upset in my routine disturbing.

I licked the fur on my shoulders, then looked back at the new man's closed glass doors. On a sudden urge, I stood up on my hind legs and pushed on the doors to see if they would part. Finding that they would not, I dropped on all fours and meowed loudly in irritation. Meowing again, I tried to see past the blinds blocking my view through the doors. Any obstruction to my free passage made me all the more determined to overcome it. A cat must always be able to investigate any situation at any time, when the whim strikes. That is a hard and fast rule all humans should know and respect, but unfortunately many humans seem incapable of grasping the concept.

To my surprise, the blinds parted, revealing the man inside staring down at me. As I skittered back and turned to leap to the neighboring balcony, the doors slid open with a heavy swoosh. I stopped in my tracks to stare wide-eyed at the man with his head sticking out between the doors.

"You're back," he said, then ducked inside, leaving the doors open wide enough for me to easily pass.

I contemplated the open doors. Was it a clever trap? Did he plan to lure me inside with seeming disinterest, then do some harm to me? Just as I decided I should leave, I smelled an oddly enticing scent and saw his hand push past the gap in the doors. A very thin slice of meat fell onto the balcony floor, and his hand retreated back inside.

Cautiously I eyed the doors for signs of further movement or activity. The blinds swayed slightly but seemed to be coming to a standstill. The odor of the folded slice of meat lying at the doors drew me forward. I came close enough to sniff it, keeping an eye on the parting of the doors. The meat was incredibly

The Cat's Fancy

Gwynn E. Ambrose

tender and disappeared down my throat before I realized I had gobbled it up.

Now intrigued, I came closer to the doors. The blinds hung still, and I could hear no commotion past them. Cautiously I sniffed the doors, getting a whiff of the meat scent still lingering in the air. Rubbing my face on the edge of one door, I peered inside, just far enough to poke aside the blinds with my nose. The living area with the wonderfully enticing couch sat in relative darkness, but the kitchen area beyond seemed promising with light. I guessed the man was in the kitchen, with more of the tender meat slices awaiting me.

As my paws carried me silently toward the light, a warning from Big Buddha Pest popped into my head ... *Don't go toward the light – it's a human saying, but still well worth heeding.* No cat I knew understood what that human saying really meant, so I ignored it and proceeded toward the light...

* * * * *

Sensing he was being watched as he put his sandwich together, Cole turned and looked over shoulder to find the big black cat staring intently at him with its yellow eyes. Trying not to be unnerved by the strange familiarity of the cat, Cole smiled and said softly, "So, you liked the smoked turkey?"

The cat meowed and sat alertly in the kitchen doorway, just at the edge of the linoleum. Cole smiled. "I know you're somebody else's kitty. And I don't make a habit of feeding strays. But you're a bit insistent, and I've got plenty. So I'll make an exception." He lifted another slice of meat from the deli pack and tossed it over to the cat, who gobbled it up without delay.

"I think that's all you need for now. Don't want to spoil your dinner. I'm sure you've got something yummy waiting at home for you." He turned to put the finishing touches on his sandwich, but was surprised by the cat's insistent meowing.

"Buddy, you need to head on home. Does your owner even

know you're out, slumming in a stranger's apartment?"

The cat meowed again and got up, strolling around with seeming purposefulness as it turned toward the darkened living room. "My couch is off-limits, buddy. It's rented, and I didn't pay a pet deposit."

The cat turned and focused on him with those unnerving yellow eyes, as if he were trying to read his mind. Cole thought for a moment, then said, "Are you lost or something? Are you in some kind of trouble?" He smiled as he realized he sounded like some character on the old classic TV show, *Lassie,* asking the usual question, *'Is Timmy in the well again?'*

The cat meowed again, as if trying to tell him something important. Cole set his sandwich aside and placed a paper plate over it to create a makeshift lid to keep the bread fresh until he could return to it. "All right, I'll bite. Let's see how smart you are. Show me what you want."

The cat turned and trotted into the living room as if satisfied with Cole's attention. Cole flipped on the living room overhead light and watched the cat sidle up to his couch. "Don't even think you're going to make yourself at home here, buddy. I'm not up for that, and I know you've already got a home. Let's you and me go find out where that home of yours is. My guess is, it can't be far."

On his way to the front door, Cole grabbed his keys off the coffee table, then turned to find the cat staring at him. Motioning with his hand, he indicated the door and opened it. "Come on. You need to get back home where you belong. I'm sure somebody's missing you about now."

The big black cat trotted out the door and swerved down the hallway, as if he knew exactly where he was going. Cole followed him, wondering what the peculiar animal was up to.

Several apartments down on the right, a door opened, and an elderly lady stepped out just when the black cat passed. "Oh, you naughty kitty," she scolded. "You're out again. Kari's going to have your ornery hide!"

The Cat's Fancy

The cat stopped and did a double-take, looking up at the woman. About that time, she looked over and spotted Cole in the hallway. "You the new fella that just moved into 2G?"

Cole smiled amiably. "Yes."

"Welcome to Garden Plaza. You'll like it here. The apartments are small, but they're clean and well-maintained and affordable."

"Yes, I agree."

"And you'll enjoy the pool, I'm sure. It's summer, and there are several young women in the complex that don't know the meaning of modesty."

Cole snickered as the elderly lady held out her hand. "I'm Ida Kelsey. I take water aerobics at the Y, so you won't have to worry about catching me down there in a bathing suit."

Cole shook her hand briefly and laughed again. Looking down at the cat still contemplating Ida Kelsey with trepidation, Cole asked, "Did you say this cat belongs to someone named Kari?" *It couldn't be KariAnn Ingles – that would be too much of a coincidence! But come to think of it, the address in her personnel file did seem familiar somehow...*

"Yes. Kari Ingles."

Cole paused, wondering how he could effectively handle this potentially awkward situation.

"Sweet girl," Ida Kelsey continued, oblivious to his private concerns. "She calls that ornery little cuss Max."

"Max, huh?"

"She's in 2B. She's good about checking on me. I'm seventy-three, you know."

Cole rubbed his chin. "I wouldn't guess a day over sixty."

It was Mrs. Kelsey's turn to giggle. "You're a shameless liar, but thank you just the same."

"Well," Cole said, turning his attention back to the cat, who now sat expectantly in front of the door to 2B. "I guess I better get Max back home."

"What'd you say your name was, young man?"

"Oh, I'm sorry. Daniel J–" He caught himself. "Daniel ... um ... Cole. Everybody just calls me Cole."

"Cole. Nice meeting you. I'm sure we'll be seeing each other again."

"Yes, nice to meet you as well, Ms. Kelsey."

"Missus. But the mister's done passed."

"Sorry to hear that."

"Thank you, but that was several years ago. He was a good man, and we had a good life. I'm thankful for what the Lord has provided. You just call me Ida. Everybody does." She waved him off and closed her door behind her. "Now you better get that ornery critter back home to Miss Kari, so she can keep an eye on him. I'm off to my Bible study."

"Have a good evening, Mrs. – Ida." Cole watched the spry little woman head for the elevator, then turned his attention to the black cat parked in front of the door to Apartment 2B.

Kari Ingles. Hmm. Maybe I can use this opportunity to find out her side of the story about her dismissal from Manning Industries, without raising her suspicions about who I am and why I'm asking. I'm liable to get closer to the truth that way...

* * * * *

Kari swiped the back of her hand across her eyes as she tried to reassure Chelle over the phone. "I'll be fine. Really. I don't need any money."

Chelle ranted and raved some more about the lowlife HR department at Manning Industries, then said, "I'll have another talk with Mr. Hatchet Man, Daniel Jordensen."

"No, don't, Chelle. You've already jeopardized your position just by making him aware of you."

"Honey, he was already aware. He's the one who called me into his office to ask what was going on with you and Braswell."

"I'm sure he's looking into things, like he promised you he would."

"Yeah, like he's gonna care. *He's* got a job – to make sure other people don't. He's probably thinking you'll add nicely to his hatchet headcount."

Kari huffed, growing sorrier by the moment that she'd called Chelle. It wasn't her friend's problem that Vance – or whoever in HR – had decided to block her claim for unemployment. It was a battle she'd have to fight herself. She couldn't lean on Chelle for everything. "Look, I gotta go. I have to get up early tomorrow and go to the unemployment office to respond to that denial of benefits."

"Okay, but if they want somebody to back up your story, you call me."

"Well, first I have to find out the reason for the denial. Maybe Vance came up with something else that doesn't have anything to do with Jeff Braswell."

"But it would still be a lie. So if you need me to–"

"I'll call you. I promise."

"Okay. Just let me know what's going on."

"I will. Talk to you later. Night, Chelle."

Kari hung up the phone and turned, startled by the sound of someone knocking on her apartment door. She looked down at the paint on her shirt and ran her hands through her messy hair. She hadn't bothered to put on a bra, and she didn't know whether to dash to the bedroom and try to spruce up, or to just ignore the insistent knocking on her door. It was almost seven. Who would be at her door anyway? Maybe it was Mrs. Kelsey needing some kind of help with something in her apartment. Or maybe it was some salesman. No, salesmen wouldn't bother going door to door anymore, they'd just aggravate her by calling her on the phone.

She heard the knock again and went to the door to peer through the peephole. She was surprised to see a tall, dark-haired man standing at her door. She fluffed her ratty hair helplessly. "Uh ... uh ... just a minute. Who is it?" She scuffled around, trying to figure out what to do, knowing it was much too late to pretend no one was home.

"My name is Cole. I just moved in a couple doors down. A lady across the hall said you had a black cat called Max."

"Yes?" Kari felt a charge of fear. "What's wrong?" She glanced around, wondering where Max was, and why this strange man was asking about him.

"Well, I came to return him. Can you maybe open the door and let him in?"

"Um ... oh. Yeah, sure." Kari fumbled with the door lock and deadbolt, finally managing to swing open the door. She was stunned speechless as she found herself looking into the dark brown eyes of the very handsome man towering over her in the doorway. Max made some kind of chortling meow and slinked into the apartment past her legs, but she barely noticed.

"So, I guess that is your cat, then," the man said.

Still speechless, Kari let out a breathy sigh as she openly admired the man. Realizing she was staring with her mouth open, she touched a hand to her lower lip, absently checking for drool, and then stepped back. "I-I'm sorry, what did you say your name was? And why are you bringing Max home? Where was he?"

"Daniel Cole," he said. "Everybody calls me Cole. I just moved into the apartment down the hall. And your cat came into my apartment to admire my couch and have some lunchmeat." His sudden smile was like the annual illumination of the Christmas tree at Rockefeller Center. "Sorry if I spoiled his supper."

Kari giggled with girlish glee as she admitted, "I'm sure it's better than what I've got left to feed him."

"Got left? You ... haven't been to the store lately?" Mr. Cole prodded.

Kari realized how desperate that sounded, and blushed. "Oh, I've ... uh ... been a little preoccupied. I'll pick up his favorites tomorrow."

Mr. Cole nodded. "I've got plenty of fresh sandwich fixings, if you'd like to take advantage until you can make it to the store."

She felt her face get hotter. "Um, thank you for the offer, but really, I've got stuff here to eat. No problem. Thank you anyway, though. That's kind of you."

He laughed softly, and the deep sound of it made her whole body tingle. "Actually, my offer was purely motivated by selfishness. I just moved in, and I don't know a single person here in this apartment complex – except for Mrs. Kelsey. She seems to think a lot of you. Not so wild about your cat apparently, but she likes you." He grinned and glanced over at Max, who was sitting in the living room floor not far away, watching their exchange intently.

Kari looked at her naughty kitty and turned back to Mr. Cole. "Exactly how did Max get into your apartment?"

He shrugged. "My fault, really. I left the patio doors open to let in some fresh air, and he invited himself in."

She frowned. "He doesn't normally do that sort of thing. He ... um ... doesn't warm to strangers, and he definitely doesn't like men."

"Oh?"

"Long story." She shook her head. "What worries me is how he got outside in the first place." She started looking around.

"Maybe you've got a window cracked that you've forgotten about?" Mr. Cole offered.

Kari glanced at the gorgeous Mr. Cole, then smiled apologetically. "I'm sorry. Would you like to come in? I'm being totally rude, leaving you standing there in the doorway."

"I don't want to intrude. It looks like you're in the middle of some redecorating."

"Huh?"

"The paint on your shirt."

"Oh." She laughed and put her hands self-consciously over her breasts to mask the fact that they were naked and perking with interest under the thin fabric of her paint-spattered tee-shirt. "I was doing a little painting."

"On canvas," Mr. Cole said knowingly.

"Yeah." She stepped back. "Have a seat. Would you like something to drink, a soda or water, or ... I'm afraid I don't have much on hand right now–"

"Because you'll be going to the store tomorrow."

"Right. Right."

"I've got plenty of drinks on hand to go with the sandwiches at my place – assuming you'll agree to take me up on the impromptu dinner offer. I promise, I'm not a hard sell, but I would like to find out a bit about Baltimore from somebody who's been here longer than a week."

Kari blushed again. "I'm kind of a home-body, but I can tell you a few hot spots that my girlfriend Raschelle knows about. Her nickname is Hot Chocolate. I'm just Pasty White Bread."

Mr. Cole laughed. "So, Hot Chocolate gets around?"

"Well, I didn't mean it like that exactly, but–"

"Sorry, no insult intended."

"Chelle's really a classy gal, and she's a very good friend. She'd do anything for you, and be there in a heartbeat if you were in a tight spot."

"That's the kind of friend everyone would like to have."

Kari nodded her head, starting to tear up as she thought about her own tight spot again. She turned away.

"So, you'll take me up on my sandwich offer? Sorry it's not steak and champagne, but I haven't had a chance to get a grill yet."

Kari managed to laugh as she swiped her fingers across her eyes. "Sandwiches sound fine. Let me kind of freshen up a bit." She turned and headed for her bedroom, then turned back and added, "Have a seat. I'll only be a moment. And thank you for bringing Max home."

She dipped down and stroked Max on the head as he sat like a statue, watching Mr. Cole. "Naughty boy!" she reprimanded, "sneaking into someone else's apartment. What's wrong with you?"

She straightened and, as an afterthought, looked at Mr.

THE CAT'S FANCY

GWYNN E. AMBROSE

Cole and warned, "Oh, and don't let him freak you out. He plays staring contests with everyone. And ... um ... don't take your shoes off."

Mr. Cole cocked his handsome head. "Now that's a shoe story you're going to have to tell me!" He sat down easily on her modern red couch, looking sexy in his pin-striped casual shirt and jeans.

She rolled her eyes. "I don't know if you'll want to hear *that* story. Just heed my warning, and you should be safe." Looking back at Mr. Cole once more to make sure she wasn't hallucinating, she turned and hurried to her bedroom, knowing Max would keep an eye on him. *Good old Max!*

She closed the door to her bedroom and peeled off her painting clothes, quickly replacing them with what she hoped was a more appealing casual ensemble of jeans and tee-shirt. Why she even bothered, she didn't know, except that she felt an instant attraction to this Daniel Cole. Her instincts about men were usually atrocious, but Max seemed to like him – he'd actually led him here. She giggled at the phrase, *look what the cat dragged in.* And so that had to count for something.

She hurried to the bathroom to see what she could do with her face and hair, and was shocked at how awful she looked. Her eyes were still slightly red-rimmed, and her hair was an absolute disaster. She was embarrassed she'd allowed a hunk like Mr. Cole to catch her looking so sloppy.

She released her blonde hair from the loose, messy ponytail she'd fashioned earlier in the day, then ran a brush through it, mildly pleased with the shining results. Wetting a washcloth with cool water, she dabbed it around her face, then held it against her closed eyes to try and ease away the puffiness and redness. With a few brush strokes of mineral powder over her face, and a tiny bit of extra pink for her cheeks, she felt her pale complexion was highlighted just enough to have a natural glow without looking too made-up.

Returning to the living room, she found Mr. Cole

contemplating the large op-art painting hanging over her red couch. He turned when he heard her enter the room, and asked, "Did you happen to paint this?"

She shrugged and admitted, "I did it back when I was in college," as if that were some kind of excuse or apology. "I had it professionally reframed later, so it wouldn't look quite so tacky."

He gave her an odd look, then turned back to admire it. "I assumed it was a print you'd purchased, and didn't realize it was an original until I looked closer and noticed the very fine brush strokes. This is quite an impressive piece." He faced her and said with an amazingly straight face, "I'm guessing you sell quite a bit of your work. What galleries represent you?"

She laughed. "Fat chance. Once I got out of college, I immediately had to get a 'day job' to pay for my college loans I took out to supplement my scholarship. I haven't painted that much since. And all my relatives are sick of receiving paintings as Christmas presents, so I kind of gave up on it."

"That's a real shame. You're very talented."

She blew air out her mouth and waved dismissively. "Believe me, the world doesn't look at it as a big loss, so I don't sweat it."

He eyed the rest of her furnishings and commented, "You have a very whimsical decorating taste."

She laughed again. "*Whimsical* is a tactful way of saying what some people would call just plain weird or ugly. The red and black and white combination is usually too much for most people. My mother hates coming to my apartment. She says the whole place makes her nervous."

Mr. Cole smiled. "I like it. It's bold, decisive."

"Another reason my mother thinks it's weird, because she says that style definitely doesn't suit me."

"She thinks you're not bold and decisive?"

Kari shrugged. "Guilty as charged."

"But you do clean up nice." His eyes quickly roamed over her, causing him to beam with what appeared to be open appreciation. Kari blushed.

"Ready for that sandwich?"

"Okay, but I can't stay long. I have to get up early tomorrow and go to the..."

"Grocery store?"

"Uh, yeah. The grocery store."

"Oh, before we go," Mr. Cole said, "I thought you'd like to know how your cat Max has been getting out." He walked over to the small living room window Kari left curtained all the time. "Looks like I was right about the partially open window."

When he pulled back the drapes, Max let out a decidedly disgruntled meow. Kari moved in to take a closer look. Sure enough, the window was open just far enough for Max to slip through. She saw the bent screen and grimaced.

"He's probably been doing this for a while," Mr. Cole said.

Kari turned to Max. "You are a very naughty kitty!" Max meowed his displeasure at her. "You stay here while Mr. Cole and I–"

"Just Cole, not 'Mister.' And no reason Max can't come along too. He's already been in my place twice."

"Twice!"

Cole laughed. "I think he's taken a real liking to my couch – and my lunchmeat selection."

CHAPTER 8

Investigation

"Make yourself comfortable," Cole said as he opened his door for Kari and her cat, who trotted beside her like a short black shadow. He closed the door, then glanced aside, noticing the stack of empty boxes he'd meant to take down to the dumpster. "Don't mind the mess. I'm still unpacking." He tossed his keys on the coffee table, then looked to see Kari surveying his apartment with appreciation.

"This is ... nice," she said. "I should take decorating lessons from you."

He laughed. "Have a seat."

As soon as she sank down in the overstuffed tan couch, she let out a little moan of joy that caused a surprising twinge in his gut. "Oh, my gosh," she whispered. "This couch is heavenly. No wonder Max likes it."

At the mention of his name, Kari's cat Max made a garbled growling meow and hopped up on the couch beside his mistress. He pushed around with his paws for a few seconds, then immediately took up residence like a king reclining on his throne. Cole chuckled. "He has no problem making himself at home."

Kari shook her head as she looked down and petted her cat. "Really, I don't know what's gotten into him. He usually doesn't act this ... relaxed ... around ... around someone he's just met."

"Apparently I have – or at least my new couch has – that effect on people," Cole said, smiling. "You like mayonnaise, mustard, lettuce, pickles?"

The Cat's Fancy

Gwynn E. Ambrose

Kari's eyes widened as she pushed herself forward. "Oh, jeez, I'm such a slob. Let me help—"

Cole put up a hand. "You're my guest. Relax. It'll only take a second to get things ready, then I'll give you a holler. I don't have any trays yet, so we'll have to eat in the kitchen."

"But I want to help."

He laughed. "Really, I'm a big boy, and I can do it by myself. I'm used to it. I insist you sit back and take it easy."

Reluctantly Kari sat back in the couch as ordered. She stroked her cat sitting satisfied beside her. Right away the tension in her face eased.

"What would you like to drink? Soda, iced tea, water, beer, wine, milk?"

"Whatever you're having with your sandwich is fine with me."

Smiling, Cole strolled into the kitchen. He washed his hands and uncovered the sandwich he'd made for himself. As he quickly built a second identical sandwich for Kari, he found himself thinking about her in a less professional and more personal mode that surprised and actually disturbed him.

He knew he had no business becoming emotionally involved with this young woman, considering his position and her history with Manning Industries. But the reality of meeting her in person on non-business turf immediately made him suspicious of the story told about her by Jeff Braswell and supported by Gerald Vance. Those two painted a completely different picture of the woman sitting in his living room, and their portrait was definitely not a good likeness. He needed more information to build his case to properly handle the situation, and a casual little chat over sandwiches might be just the ticket.

* * * * *

"This is the best sandwich," Kari mumbled with her mouth full, "that I've had in ... I don't know when." She chewed and swallowed, then said more clearly, "You should open a sandwich shop, Cole."

He gave her a sidelong look with those dreamy brown eyes of his. "Funny you should mention that. I've been toying with the idea for years of opening my own restaurant."

Kari stared at him across the round wooden dinette table. "Really? Are you a chef? Do you cook professionally? Is that what brought you to Baltimore?"

The deep rumbling sound of his laughter caught her right in the gut, and she fidgeted uncomfortably, trying to ignore her instant and growing attraction to this man. She had no business falling for him – he could have a wife and kids tucked away somewhere, for all she knew.

"No, a job transfer brought me here, but it's temporary. I don't know for how long."

"What do you do?"

He looked at her again, his bedroom eyes boring deep, as if he could see past all the pretense and social niceties, straight into her core, the heart of her needy soul. She focused on her sandwich, trying to hide the rawness inside her. It shocked her to realize suddenly how lonely she was and how much she craved some genuine male companionship.

"I'm ... an asset manager," he said finally.

She looked up when she heard the hesitation in his answer. "What the heck is that?"

He laughed again. "Just a fancy doubletalk title for a really unpleasant job."

"Hopefully it pays well."

He shrugged. "I can't complain, except for the frequent travel. That was the trigger for my breakup with my last girlfriend."

"Oh, sorry," she said, trying to hide her giddiness. *So he's not married. At least not at the moment.*

"Trust me, no love was lost in that relationship. I was actually relieved to have an excuse to leave."

The Cat's Fancy

Gwynn E. Ambrose

She eyed him cautiously as she took another bite of her sandwich. *A commitment phobia?*

"Oh, don't get me wrong," he reassured, as if he could read her apprehension. "It's not that I don't want to settle down. It's just that Beth was not the one I would have chosen to settle down with."

"Then why—"

"Innocent bystander caught in a planned arrangement. A so-called friend of mine fixed me up with her, and I wasn't quick enough to figure out how to get out gracefully before she'd moved in with her high-maintenance demands and yappy little dog."

Kari curled her upper lip in dismay.

"Exactly. Not that I'd never want a dog. I'd just never want one of *those* dogs."

At the mention of the word *dog*, Max growled a rumbling meow of dissatisfaction. Kari looked over to find him seated in his usual statue pose on the floor, looking up intently at her and Cole. He'd had another helping of lunchmeat, so she knew he couldn't be hungry. Her suspicion grew that he understood what 'dog' meant – along with a lot of other human words. He stared at her, unblinking, as if to telepathically transmit to her his disdainful announcement, *'Yes, I understand everything you say. And your point is...?'*

"So tell me about this shoe story involving your cat," Cole prodded.

At the sound of Cole's tantalizing voice, Kari managed to pull her attention free of Max's hypnotizing stare. "Um ... well..." She laughed nervously. "Really, it's sort of embarrassing."

"The best kind of story. Spill."

She laughed again, eyeing this man with renewed curiosity. He was very different from the typical date material she was used to. Handsome and self-confident, he actually seemed to care about the needs of others beyond his own exclusive self-interest. He made pleasant small talk and appeared to be interested in what she had to say. And he'd openly accepted her cat – a previously one-hundred-percent effective man repellant. She wanted to pinch herself to make sure she hadn't just dreamed up Daniel Cole as part of an elaborate hallucination to fill her boring, empty life. He almost sounded too good to be true.

"Earth to Kari..." Cole said.

Kari snapped out of her little reverie, laughing to cover her embarrassment. "Well, okay, if you insist. But really, this is not a story I should be telling anyone. It's just too ... oh, it makes me look like a complete fool."

"I won't hold it against you. I promise." He smiled fetchingly.

Kari grabbed her glass and took a big swallow of tea. "All right," she said, instantly regretting her willingness to let this man talk her into spilling personal information about herself. "My boss ... well, I guess I should say my *former* boss–"

"Former?"

She winced. "Yeah. I ... kind of ... got escorted off the job last week."

"Fired. Ouch."

She winced again and nodded. "I'm not going to the grocery store tomorrow. I'm going to the unemployment office to contest the denial of my benefits."

Cole gave her an odd, dark look. "When were you notified of the denial?"

"Today."

He scowled. "So, you were fired for just cause?"

She shrugged. "If I was, nobody bothered to tell me which cause it was. I'm going in tomorrow to find out what kind of trumped-up excuse that horse's rear in Human Resources used to keep me from getting my benefits."

Cole looked aside for a second, as if he were angry. Facing her, he said, "I'm really sorry to hear about your job troubles."

She waved dismissively. "It's not your problem. I've got my application in at several places, and I'll get the unemployment benefits thing straightened out soon enough. I mean, don't they have to come up with some kind of proof to keep me from getting my benefit checks?"

Cole nodded solemnly. "I think they'd have to show documented history of problematic, potential dangerous, or illegal behavior, and provide evidence of attempts to counsel you or otherwise help you to manage the situation. Without that kind of documentation, the denial of benefits would be nothing more than a nuisance attempt to discourage you, in hopes that you wouldn't challenge the denial. In any case, if you challenge it, and they can't back up their denial with real documented support, your benefits will be delayed only until the benefits office can make a determination based on what evidence has been offered from both sides."

Kari stared at him in surprise. "You sound like some kind of expert on this stuff."

He managed a calm smile. "I've had a little personal experience with it."

"Oh," she said, fidgeting uncomfortably. "Guess I'm not the first or last person in the world to be let go from a job." As she looked down at her empty plate and near-empty glass on the table, she mumbled, "Well, thanks for the sandwich. It was great. But it's getting late, and I probably should be getting back–"

"Not before I hear the shoe story," Cole prodded warmly. "I don't want to walk into your apartment sometime and get blindsided by your cat." He looked over at Max, who stared back with the supreme aloofness only a cat can pull off successfully.

"Really," Kari protested, "I've already said too much and..."

"Nonsense. I'm sorry if I made you uncomfortable asking questions about your job, but–"

"No, no, it's not that, it's just..."

"More tea?" Cole interrupted, reaching for the pitcher.

"Half a glass."

As he poured, he smiled at her and said, "So give me the

short version, and we'll call it an evening."

She shook her head in dismay. "Okay, but it's really stupid. Really. It's also the reason, I think, that I got fired."

"Oh?" Cole set the pitcher down and sat back in his chair, waiting expectantly for her to continue.

She took a big breath and launched into the back-story. "My boss – supervisor at the time – was this stupid jerk who didn't know a thing about his job. He got hired about six months ago because he was somebody's nephew or something. And I got stuck training him to do the job that I was doing when the last supervisor left – retired."

"And you felt he was incompetent and unsuited for the job that you should have had?"

"No, no," she said, waving a hand in the air. "I know it sounds like I was jealous because he got the job instead of me, but that's not the point." She shrugged. "I wasn't the only one who thought he was incompetent. But regardless, I tried to get along with him and show him how everything was supposed to be done. I mean, I wasn't making the hiring decisions, so I didn't have much choice. I really did try to work with him, but he'd do things wrong and then blame it on me, and try to make it look like suddenly I didn't know what I was doing. There was no getting along with him. He was awful to everyone – especially me – almost like he was deliberately trying to make us all so miserable, we'd all quit so the company wouldn't have to pay us unemployment. He managed to get rid of several people that complained, but I couldn't afford to just walk out on my job, so..."

"So you kept quiet and put up with his crap."

"Yeah."

"And then ... something changed?"

Kari sighed. "Yeah. The weekend before I got fired, he called me at home on the phone and started going on about how sorry he was about being such a jerk at work, and would I please let him make it up to me so we could start off new, and try to be friends." She shook her head. "He wanted to come over to my place and watch a movie and eat popcorn. I thought it was really weird, and I was suspicious, but I didn't want to act like I wasn't a 'team player,' so I told him he could come over for a while if he wanted to."

Kari caught Cole staring at her with a simmering look, as if he were getting angrier by the second. She didn't understand the source of his displeasure, and hoped he wasn't judging her. "I warned you this was really stupid. I know I should have just told him to go jump in the lake, but really, I didn't know what to say. He caught me off guard, and he sounded so convincing about wanting to be friends and get along better. And I thought, well, maybe it would make work a little more tolerable, so why not try to get along with him or whatever. Actually, I was afraid he'd be even worse to me at work if I so no. So..."

She sighed miserably. "So he came over to my apartment, and I found a movie he said he hadn't seen that sounded interesting, and then I went to the kitchen to make the popcorn. He asks to use my bathroom, and the next thing I know, he's hollering for me to come back to my bedroom."

Cole shifted forward in his chair, as if he were bracing for a fight. Kari stopped and stared at him, startled. "Go on," he urged in a low, even tone that almost sounded menacing.

"Well ... I thought the toilet was stopped up or something. Max is always dropping his toys in the toilet – he likes to watch them float so he can bat them around in the water. Sometimes they get waterlogged and sink." She shrugged, embarrassed to have to admit Max played with his toys in the toilet. "At least it forces me to keep the toilet clean."

Cole blinked his eyes, as if that admission had pulled him out of his smoldering mood. A smile spread slowly across his face. "Go on..."

"So I go in there, expecting to have to use the plunger, and dreading the whole mess." She threw up her hands. "The last thing I expected was to see my boss standing there in his tidy whities and socks!"

Cole stared at her in astonishment. "He had taken his clothes off?"

Kari nodded. "Shirt, pants, shoes. Everything but his socks and underwear."

"And that's where Max comes in, why you said he doesn't take to men very well."

Kari nodded again. "Max followed me in there, and wasted no time peeing in his very expensive tennis shoes."

Cole burst out laughing and continued for nearly a minute. When he calmed himself, he said, still chuckling, "So ... I'm guessing it didn't take your *former* boss too awful long to put his clothes back on and vacate the premises."

Kari sighed. "Max has pulled similar stunts on every guy who's ever dared enter my apartment – except for my dad and my brother."

Still chuckling, Cole offered, "Maybe Max doesn't think much of your choice in men."

"Obviously not. The last guy who came to visit was sitting on the couch with me, trying to ... um ... get friendly. And Max went over to his food bowl, gobbled up everything that was there, then came over and jumped up in the guy's lap and vomited on him."

Cole burst out laughing again.

About that time, Kari looked over to find that Max had disappeared from the kitchen. "Oh. Oh, I need to go find him before..." She jumped up from the table and scurried into the living room, but didn't see her errant cat anywhere. "Max? Maxi, where are you. Come out here right now, Max!"

She slapped her thigh with the palm of her hand and repeatedly called to him. Cole quickly joined her in the living room, presumably to aid in the search. She looked up at him in apologetic desperation. "I'm sorry. He's hard to control sometimes."

Cole chuckled. "He's a cat."

The Cat's Fancy

Precisely on cue, as if he'd timed his reappearance, Max meowed and came strolling out of the hall bathroom just off the living room – with a train of toilet paper dragging behind his left rear leg.

Cole roared with laughter, barely able to manage, "He's potty-trained too?"

Mortified, Kari rushed over to her ill-behaved cat. "Maxi, you bad, bad kitty! You do not play with the toilet paper in other people's homes! Bad kitty!" She pulled the trailing toilet paper off the back of his foot, where it had snagged on a claw, only to realize it was also still attached to the roll in the bathroom. Grabbing Max up in her arms, she turned to Cole. "I'm so sorry. He ... I really can't take him anywhere!"

Still chuckling, Cole walked over and picked up the limp ribbon of toilet paper strung down the hall. "Don't worry about it. I'll roll back up, and it'll be almost good as new."

Squeezing Max as he wiggled in her arms, Kari growled, "Bad, bad kitty!" She looked at Cole and winced apologetically. "I need to take him home before he decides to get into something else. Thanks again for the sandwich and the conversation." She headed for the door. "Sorry about your toilet paper. And if you're brave enough, next time you can come over to my place to have dinner. I'm not a very good cook, but I can manage a pizza without burning it – usually."

Wrestling with Max, she got the door open and then tossed him out in the hallway. He trotted toward her apartment. She turned back and found Cole had followed her to the door. "Thanks again, Cole. And sorry for–"

"Don't worry about it," he said softly, almost intimately.

His tone made her blush. "Well ... uh ... g'night then." She stepped back, forcing herself further into the hallway so she would have to leave.

"Good night, Kari," he said from the open doorway. "And good luck tomorrow on your ... trip into town. I'm sure things will work out for you."

"I hope so," she said over her shoulder as she took one last look at the man she figured would never dare step foot in her apartment ever again. As he closed his door, she sighed and turned to follow her abominable cat to her apartment. "I hope you're happy with yourself, El Destructo, because I'm sure not."

Max stopped long enough to look up at her and meow as if he had accomplished something very important and couldn't understand why she wasn't just as pleased as he was. She shook her head and unlocked the door to her apartment. "Get in there, Romance Wrecker. At the rate we're going, I'll end up the resident Crazy Cat Lady – you know, the one that lives alone and talks to her cat?"

Max meowed as if in total agreement, then slithered into the apartment, apparently quite satisfied to be back home.

CHAPTER 9

Confrontation

Kari awoke with a grunt when Max pounced on her stomach with the full weight of his fifteen pounds. She made an unfocused swipe at him with a leaden arm, but he yowled and jumped off the bed, too quick for her.

Distracted by the blaring beeping of the alarm and her full bladder about to explode after Max's sucker-punch, she wrangled herself to a sitting position and then slammed her hand down on the alarm. When she saw the time – she must have slept through the alarm for an amazing thirty minutes – she bolted up from bed and raced into the bathroom.

Forty-five minutes later, she was on her way out the door to face off at the unemployment office.

* * * * *

I sniffed disdainfully at the day-old, leftover dry food in my bowl. Kari had changed the water, but she had not refilled my food bowl. Why?

I jumped up onto the kitchen counter and reached for the cabinet door where she kept the sacks of dry cat food. I knew the canned goodies were gone, but was surprised to find no sack of dry cat food either. The cabinet looked dismally spacious and empty. The few items remaining were cans and boxes of no interest to me. Not bothering to sniff them, I jumped down to the floor with a yowl of displeasure and worry.

Why hadn't Kari gone to the place she called 'the store'? It was always exciting when she dragged sacks of things into the kitchen. I would quickly and eagerly investigate everything while she tried to put the items away. But I couldn't recall having done that in quite some time. Surely she was due to bring another set of bags home from 'the store.' Perhaps that is where she was headed off to in such a rush this morning. She realized we were in dire need of food, and she had wasted no time going to get some to replenish the cabinets.

Satisfied with that determination, I made my way back to my food bowl. Selecting carefully, I forced myself to chew on a few pieces of stale cat food, just to tide me over until Kari returned with new food from 'the store.'

* * * * *

"W-Well, Mr. Jordensen," Gerald Vance stuttered, surprised by Cole's demand. "I hate to disagree, but I really don't think that would be in the best interest of Manning Industries. VP Kendall and I have already discussed the situation, and he agreed that—"

"Vance," Cole growled, towering over the man's desk to physically intimidate him, "I don't give a flip what you and Kendall think, because it's obvious to me neither of you has anyone's best interest at heart here – except for your own and those of your cronies and yes-men. Do I need I remind you who is in charge of this district office now?"

"No, sir, Mrs. Jordensen," Vance whispered.

"Good." Cole straightened and stepped back from the desk to give Vance some room to breathe easier. "Make the call now, and say exactly what I told you – nothing more and nothing less. Understand?"

"Yes, sir."

"And make sure you speak directly with the caseworker handling this particular claim."

The Cat's Fancy

Gwynn E. Ambrose

Vance sat in his desk chair, staring stupidly at Cole. "She could sue Manning Industries and cost the company–"

"You idiot! Are you really that stupid? If she's denied her unemployment benefits, even temporarily, she'll be forced to sue just to get what's rightfully due her! By denying her unemployment benefits, you're actually setting the company up to get sued!"

"But ... but it's just her word against Braswell's."

Cole shook his head in amazement. "You're forgetting phone records. Braswell can't go back and doctor his phone bill. He called her, didn't he? Not the other way around."

Vance lowered his gaze. He didn't answer.

Cole glared at him, feeling his blood boil. How could the man be so stupid to try this kind of scam? And just to get rid of someone who wasn't a real threat to anyone! "You know," he said in the smoothest, calmest conversational tone he could manage, "I've seen a lot of office politics and petty turf wars in the time I've been with Manning. And none of it was pretty. A lot of people lost their jobs for no reason, and cost the company millions in squandered resources. And for what? So some little tinhorn feudal lord could gather his forces and duke it out for control ... control ... control of *what?*"

Vance looked up slowly, like a condemned man about to walk the last mile.

"That's what I don't understand. All you stupid people with your fancy titles and big money, you throw your weight around and play king of the mountain, trying to push everyone else off to prove you are top dog. Top dog of *what?*"

Cole shook his head. "When you're done destroying everything to get at someone you're trying to crush, there's nothing left. You've destroyed the company and its ability to support itself. You've just torn everything up so it won't work anymore, and can't be fixed. And then somebody like me has to come in and clean up your mess."

He turned and headed for the door. Grabbing the doorknob,

he turned back and gave Vance a parting scowl. "I know you and Kendall thought by getting rid of anyone who complained or opposed you would protect your jobs. But look what you've done. You've brought in some untrustworthy weasel who browbeat and abused the good employees here, just to get them to quit so they wouldn't draw on Manning's unemployment account reserves. And you thought you were doing Manning a favor by cutting costs. But what you ended up doing was crippling the workforce so that there wasn't enough qualified staff left to handle legitimate workload. And then you let that little weasel stoop to sexual harassment, actually thinking you could get away with it without consequence?"

Cole looked at his hand gripping the doorknob. He knew exactly what needed to be done here, and he had no qualms about it. He twisted the doorknob and cracked the door as he locked back over his should at Vance and said, "Make that call. Now. Just as I instructed you to."

"Yes. Yes, sir. Right now, sir," Vance said in a jittery voice, reaching for the phone.

Cole swung the door open and slammed it shut behind him, then paced down the hallway without looking at anyone, even though he knew several people were staring, curious about the exchange he'd had with HR Director Vance. *Former* HR Director Vance.

Cole grabbed his cell phone and called Security, requesting that two officers go directly to Vance's office, wait for him to complete a phone call he might be in the middle of, then escort him directly off the premises. Cole wanted Vance's office security-locked to keep anyone from accessing it until he had a chance to go through all the records himself. And under no circumstances was Vance to take any papers or files or computer storage devices out of the office with him. Cole authorized a strip search if Vance even pretended to try to take anything with him.

Smiling, Cole ended the call and sat down in his office to think of his next move. *Well, at least Kari Ingles will get some*

The Cat's Fancy
Gwynn E. Ambrose

unemployment benefits now, until she can find another job.

* * * * *

"What do you mean, you can't tell me what the reasons for the denial are?" Kari demanded.

The caseworker she'd been assigned was a tired-looking middle-aged black woman named Mrs. Johnson. Mrs. Johnson amply filled the creaking swivel office chair of her tiny cubicle overstuffed with an old computer with a CTR monitor – not one of the newer style flat ones – and mountains of papers and files stacked all over every possibly available surface, including the floor. Obviously she was overworked and under-resourced.

She gave Kari a deadpan stare, as if she were used to this kind of reaction. "Calm down, Miss Ingles. I'm not allowed to share the information in your file with you during our investigation of your case."

Kari jutted her hands in the air. "Well, how am I supposed to provide a response to ... to ... to *nothing?*"

The caseworker sighed and turned back to her desk to consult Kari's file. Kari was amazed she was able to find it in this mess. "Don't you keep all this stuff on a computer system now?"

"My computer is broken," Mrs. Johnson mumbled, with her eyes glued to the file. "And the state budget shortfall doesn't allow for a replacement. So, no, many of these files are not on a centralized system. They all have to be processed by hand, which is creating a huge backlog in claims."

She turned back to face Kari. "As a formality, and a requirement of our office, I will be asking you a series of specific question, and jotting down your responses on a form."

"Is that how I'll be responding to the denial of benefits from Manning Industries?"

"Yes."

Kari slumped as she sat in the metal folding chair crammed next to the caseworker's desk. "Okay." *Like, what other choice do I have?*

Mrs. Johnson took a ballpoint pen and poised it over the file lying open on her desk. "Did you provide false information on your original employment application for your job at Manning Industries?"

Kari frowned, confused by the question. "No." She thought back, second-guessing herself, trying to think what information might possibly have been mistakenly tagged as 'false.' She couldn't think of anything. She shook her head and repeated, "No."

Mrs. Johnson marked something in her file and proceeded to the next question. "Have you ever stolen anything from Manning Industries – office supplies, or sensitive information either in files, computer storage devices, or–"

"No!"

The caseworker glared at her. "I didn't finish the question."

"Well, I didn't steal anything, so you can mark that 'no.'"

The caseworker sighed irritably and moved to the next question and the next and the next. Kari answered all her questions truthfully, and admitted she'd arrived late to work several times, but had not been formally written up for it or otherwise officially reprimanded. She didn't count Jeff Braswell's public verbal lashings in front of other coworkers as an 'official' reprimand, just an impromptu outburst from an unprofessional jerk.

When the caseworker read her a lengthy and detailed description of sexual harassment, and explained the various nuances and typical situations as examples for comparison, Kari became a bit nervous, wondering if Chelle or someone else had made a report about Jeff coming to her house and acting inappropriately. She knew Chelle was the only person she'd told about it – well, besides her new neighbor last night. So how would anyone have known? Jeff Braswell certainly wouldn't have gone in and reported himself.

"You've stated you understand the information I've read to

you," Mrs. Johnson announced. "Now I'm going to ask you a series of questions specific to your interactions with your coworkers at Manning Industries. Are you ready?"

Kari scowled and nodded.

"Have you ever made sexually suggestive remarks to another coworker, including regarding their appearance or apparel, or behavior – or yours in reference to a coworker? Please let me know if you need me to repeat the question."

Fuming, Kari tried to keep her voice even as she said, "No, I don't need the question repeated, and no, I have never made any sexually suggestive remarks to any of my coworkers at Manning Industries – ever!"

As the caseworker marked down something in her file, Kari began to suspect that Jeff – the little weasel – had gone to HR and lied, complaining about *her* coming onto *him!*

"Have you ever touched a coworker inappropriately or without invitation or preced–"

"No!" Kari interrupted. "I've hugged some folks when they left after being fired from Manning Industries. I've shaken hands with a couple VPs. But I've never tried to feel anyone up, or put my hands on them in any way that would suggest I was interested in a sexual relationship!

"And if that lowdown dirty scumbag Jeff Braswell even pretended to suggest that I did, I've got news for you! He called me up at my house on the Saturday before I was fired and escorted out of the building on Monday. He called me up and invited himself over with some lame excuse about wanting to try to mend our work relationship and be on friendlier terms. And like an idiot, I felt like I had to let him come over, or else my job would be in even worse jeopardy than I suspected it already was.

"But I never gave him any indication, verbal or otherwise, that I was sexually interested in him or willing to have sex with him for fun or for the privilege of keeping my job. Nevertheless, he slipped into my bedroom while I was in the kitchen making popcorn, and ambushed me by calling me back to my bedroom to find him standing in his skivvies. And if my cat hadn't peed in his shoes to run that spineless weasel out of my apartment first, I would have called the cops on him and had him hauled to jail, or at least forcibly escorted out of my home!"

Clutching her purse in her lap, Kari shot up from the folding chair, and it toppled backward, landing on a precarious stack of files that dominoed into another stack and another. "If that's what this denial of benefits is all about – some bogus claim that I made inappropriate advances toward Jeff Braswell, then you can put in your report that the inappropriate advance was initiated by him toward me, and I was fired before I had a chance to file an official sexual harassment complaint!"

She huffed and jerked on the hem of her blouse to straighten it. "And I'm going to go find a lawyer right now to go ahead and file that complaint. Because I've been given no reason for being fired, and no reason for being denied benefits, so I can only assume that these events are all related to that one uninvited and unwelcome sexual advance from my sleazy, lying, underhanded former supervisor, Jeff Braswell. And here's the proof: he still has *his* job, while I'm unemployed and can't even get my measly unemployment checks! So what does that tell you?"

She gave the caseworker a parting glare and said, "I trust that pretty much covers all your questions?"

Mrs. Johnson, staring at her in stupefaction, was interrupted by the ringing of her desk phone before she could formulate an answer. She put up a plump index finger and said, as she reached for her phone, "Hold on, please, Miss Ingles, and don't leave. We're not finished yet."

Mrs. Johnson answered the call while Kari stood nearby, waiting impatiently. As far as Kari was concerned, they were done. She was done. What else needed to be – could be – said?

With a peculiar look on her face, Mrs. Johnson hung up the phone and turned to Kari. Smiling oddly, she said, "Yes, Miss Ingles. I think that pretty much covers everything. I have all the information I need to make a final determination on your appeal. I don't anticipate any further trouble from Manning Industries regarding your case."

Confused by the sudden turn of events, Kari scowled suspiciously. "So ... I don't have to come back here and answer any more questions or fill out any forms, and I will get my unemployment checks on schedule?"

Mrs. Johnson nodded, adding, "As long as you report online as directed."

"Good." Kari stuck out her hand. "Thank you for your time and your help with this."

The woman shook her hand and then said, "Best of luck on your sexual harassment suit, Miss Ingles."

Kari left the building knowing the threat of a suit was just that – an empty threat. She didn't have the money to get a lawyer, and she suspected Manning Industries knew that. So why the sudden turn of events? Did Mrs. Johnson just feel sorry for her or believe her story over Manning's? Or did it have something to do with that cryptic phone call she received just as Kari was preparing to leave? Maybe Chelle had gone in to see the Hatchet Man again, and convinced him to step in. Whatever the reason, Kari knew somehow someone had intervened on her behalf to help her out, and she was thankful. Now she could go to the grocery store and not worry about how she would make her next rent payment. And Max could enjoy his favorite treats again.

CHAPTER 10

Cooking up Romance

Back at his apartment, Cole gloried in a day at work well spent. As he changed his clothes, he tried to concentrate on what he'd fix for supper tonight, and then immediately thought of Kari. He wanted to invite her to dinner and fix something extra special, but he worried that any encouragement of a relationship would just get him further in hot water.

As he pulled an old faded tee-shirt over his head, he reminded himself of all the reasons why he needed to stay clear of Kari Ingles.

The first and most important was that she lived here in Baltimore, and his job was just temporary. The way he was cleaning house at Manning, it wouldn't be long until he'd have the place in top shape and ready to turn over to some in-house flunky Manning was looking to slot into a regional director position. Cole knew he held the title only until he got the office complex running reasonably well on its own again. And then ... and then he didn't know what his future held. Manning might not actually have a use for him anymore.

In front of the mirror, he raked his fingers through his thick hair, ruffled from the tee-shirt.

The next reason on his Stay Away From Kari list was the fact that she had a history with Manning, and he'd lied about his connection to Manning. It would only be a matter of time before Kari and her friend Raschelle compared notes and figured out that Daniel Cole in Garden Plaza 2G was Daniel Cole Jordensen,

The Cat's Fancy

Gwynn E. Ambrose

Hatchet Man at Manning Industries. He didn't know what kind of fallout would result from that revelation and realization, but he knew it wouldn't be good. Kari would surely hate him for lying to her by not telling her everything up front – and especially for fudging on his real name. It all looked so underhanded and sneaky – and it was. He couldn't deny that.

He strolled into his living room softly lit by the early evening sun and plopped down on his cushy couch. It was heavenly, just as Kari had pronounced it to be. But that didn't make any of his growing personal problems easier to handle.

The third and final reason to stay away from Kari was ... he really liked her. And because he really liked her, he didn't want to get attached to her and then have to give her up because he was moving again or she hated liars or ... or ... he just didn't want to hurt her, or hurt himself. And he'd already set things up perfectly to do that. It would take a miracle to undo the damage he'd already done just with one little white lie – by not telling her who he really was in the very beginning. And even if he fessed up now, it would be too late, because he'd already told the lie. And he knew he couldn't base a good solid relationship on a lie.

He shook his head and then leaned back into the couch, trying to bury his troubles and his worries in the thickly cushioned pub-style back. Closing his eyes, he decided to take a short nap – until he heard the insistent meow outside his patio doors.

He stood up and looked through the open blinds to see Kari's cat pawing at his doors, leaving smeary prints on the glass. He walked over and opened the doors. Before he could say anything, the cat trotted in, grumbling a disgruntled meow as he headed for the couch and jumped onto it.

Cole chuckled. "Well, yeah, go ahead and make yourself at home, why don't you?"

Max looked at him and meowed, then settled into the middle cushion of the couch, right where Cole had been sitting a moment before. "Ground rules, buddy. Don't sit in my seat. It's rude, and I own the place – at least make payments on it – not you."

Max let out a half-hearted yowl and settled his head on his paws, as if he really didn't care who paid for what. He looked like he was down for the night.

"Oh, no. Don't you go and get all comfy and settled in. You don't live here." Walking closer to him, Cole shook his head. "Does your very pretty mistress know where you are right now?"

Max's only response was to purr loudly as he snuggled deeper into his spot on the couch.

Cole rubbed the back of his neck, wondering what he was supposed to do now – leave the cat be, or call Kari? Suddenly his face lit up, and he winked at the napping cat. "Thanks, buddy. Maybe I can figure out a way to make this work after all – with your help."

Approaching the cat carefully, Cole rounded the coffee table and stood near the couch. "Max," he said softly, "I've got to go down the hall for a minute, but I'll be right back."

The cat never stirred or made any acknowledgment. Cole watched his midsection move regularly as the cat breathed in seeming deep sleep. Cautiously he touched his fingertips to the cat's back. "Max?"

With a cat-like grunt, Max looked up with a start and stared back over his shoulder at Cole. Entranced by the sleek, velvety softness of Max's fur, Cole dared to stroke a palm over his body. The cat didn't stir, but instead started purring. "I have to go down the hall for a minute," Cole repeated, feeling stupid for talking to the cat because he was certain the animal neither understood nor cared what he said. "I'll be right back. I hope your lovely mistress is at home and will answer the door..."

Max, still purring, laid his head back down and closed his yellow eyes. Cole left him on the couch and headed for the door to his apartment.

* * * * *

73

THE CAT'S FANCY   GWYNN E. AMBROSE

Just finished putting the groceries away, Kari wondered why Max hadn't been underfoot trying to sniff and paw and open everything as she pulled stuff out of her grocery bags.

She folded her reusable cloth bags and stuck them in the kitchen drawer, trying to figure out where in the world Max was – and then remembered the open window in the living room. She'd meant to close it last night after Cole showed it to her, but then of course she let herself get distracted by his commanding presence, and she'd completely forgot about the window.

Deciding she should take care of that now, she headed into the living room, then stopped. Maybe ... maybe it was good that Max had an outlet. But no, she didn't want him out roaming at night, getting into mischief, or fights with other animals, or worse – getting hit by a car or picked up by someone. Anything could happen to him. He could get trapped in something or–

She had to stop thinking of the possibilities, or she'd drive herself nuts. The fear of something happening to Max made her charge toward the window, until she realized he was probably outside right now. If she closed it, he'd have no way back into the apartment. With a heavy sigh, she decided to leave it open until she knew for sure he was safely inside the apartment where he belonged. Then she'd close it and make sure he only went outside when *she* decided it was appropriate.

As she stood in her living room, still wearing the casual dressy outfit she'd put on to go to the unemployment office, she heard someone knocking on her apartment door. Immediately she thought of Cole, and her heart raced, but she forced herself to calm down and not run to answer the door. It was probably Mrs. Kelsey. She just couldn't afford to let herself get her hopes up about Cole. He was charming and handsome and attentive, but that didn't mean he was interested.

When she swung the door open, she was surprised to see the man of her thoughts standing right before her, as if her thoughts had conjured him. "Cole," she breathed. "What ... what a surprise."

He smiled. "I would have called, but I don't have your number, and you're not listed in the directory."

"Oh, yeah," she said, trying to keep her mind on the conversation and her eyes off his bulky biceps straining against the sleeves of his worn olive green tee-shirt. He looked oh-so-sexy, yet casually relaxed. "That was ... uh ... my parents' idea when I moved here They were kind of paranoid about me moving so far away."

"Far away?"

"From Wisconsin. I came here to Maryland originally to go to school, and then, you know, had to look for a job when I graduated, so..." She shrugged, then remembered her manners. "Oh, you want to come in?" She stepped out of the way to let him into the apartment.

Laughing, she said, "I guess it's my turn to feed you. You'll be glad to know I made it to the grocery store – for real. I have plenty of frozen pizzas on hand."

"Mmm ... sounds ... um ... real appetizing." Cole closed the door behind him. "So, your appointment went well?"

"Yeah. Amazingly." She shook her head and sat down on the edge of one of her two black and white chairs as he stood off to the side, slightly behind her. "At first I thought it was going to be another one of those government runaround situations, especially when I saw the mess my caseworker's office was in. Her computer didn't even work.

"And then she went through this time-consuming routine, asking me a lot of questions, and said she couldn't tell me anything about the case, like the reason I was denied benefits. And then when I was about done and ready to leave, she gets this phone call, and all of a sudden, everything's okay. It was really weird."

Shaking her head again, Kari got up from the chair to find Cole standing silhouetted in the late afternoon light, looking at her like some dark angel. "I know somebody must have stepped in somehow and done something," she said, "but I don't have a clue who or how."

"I wouldn't worry about it if I were you," Cole advised. "Just be glad everything worked out. I'm happy for you."

She giggled with relief. It wasn't the ideal situation, but then again, maybe it was. She had enough money coming in now to make her monthly financial obligations – just barely enough – and she had free time on her hands, plus she didn't have to show up at her awful job at Manning Industries anymore. How much better could things be, at least for the time being? She giggled again. "I feel like a huge weight's been lifted off my chest, and I can breathe again. Oh, I know I'm going to have to find another job, but at least this gives me the time to do it, and hopefully find something not so bad."

Sighing, she shook her head. "Manning Industries wasn't that bad of a place to work at first ... until ... well, I can't really put my finger on the exact moment everything started getting bad, but when Jeff Braswell came to work there, things *really* got bad in a hurry."

Still standing tall and manly, silhouetted in the darkening evening light filtering into her living room, Cole looked even more like an avenging angel when he said in a sinister tone, "I wouldn't worry about Jeff Braswell anymore, if I were you. I have a feeling he's going to get what's coming to him very soon."

She tilted her head, curious about the knowing tone of his pronouncement, when he added in a much lighter vein, "Oh, I almost forgot. The reason I came over here was to tell you your cat's asleep on my couch."

"Oh, no, I–"

"It's not a problem, really," he interrupted, putting up a hand to calm her. "I just wanted you to know where he is."

She scrunched her face apologetically. "I forgot to close that darn window last night. But I'll do it for sure, as soon as I get his furry black butt back in here. I'll go over right now and–"

"Have dinner with me," Cole interrupted, putting words in

her mouth.

"Well, really, I think it's my turn to cook."

"But you'd rather have brazed chicken breast with portabella mushrooms than frozen pizza, wouldn't you?"

Kari blinked her eyes in astonishment. "Uh ... sure ... but I'm not cooking that!"

"You're right," Cole said, walking closer to her. "I am. I have a delicious recipe I'd like to try on you, and it doesn't really take that long to prepare."

She snickered. "It would take me forever, and it still wouldn't be edible – even for a starving coyote."

"Not to worry. I'm a little more effective in the kitchen than that. I think I've moved beyond coyote cuisine so that my cooking is actually suitable for human consumption."

Kari laughed. "Let me change clothes, and this time I'll see if I can help out and maybe learn something."

"Okay, take your time. I'll go back over and get things started."

As Cole dashed out of her apartment, Kari wondered what had made her luck change so dramatically. Maybe getting fired from that crappy job was the best thing that could have happened to her. And meeting a man who loves to cook ... how could life get any better?

Thank goodness Max was a naughty, nosy kitty. If it hadn't been for him, she might not have met Cole before some other lucky woman snapped him up!

Smiling, Kari headed for her bedroom to change clothes.

* * * * *

As Cole cross-sliced the chicken breasts and the mushrooms, he kept feeling jittery. Part of it, he knew, was the excitement of having Kari in his apartment again. But he kept thinking about their budding relationship, and how much worse it would be damaged, the longer he waited to tell her the truth about

The Cat's Fancy

Gwynn E. Ambrose

himself. He knew it would be the end of things to confess his little white lie, but if he talked fast enough, maybe he could get her to listen to his reason for lying in the first place before she turned around and walked out on him. He hadn't meant to hurt her. Really he hadn't. It was just that–

The light tapping on his apartment door signaled that his guest had arrived. He set his food preparations aside and dried his hands on a towel. Hurrying into the living room softly lit with side lamps sitting on matching tables on either end of the couch, he saw Kari's cat was still fast asleep on the couch, giving his apartment a homey feel. Smiling, he opened the door, pleased to see Kari dressed comfortably in jeans and tee-shirt that accentuated her slender, curvy figure.

She opened her mouth to say something, but he put a finger to his lips and whispered, "Shh ... somebody's still asleep on the couch."

Wide-eyed, Kari stepped through the apartment doorway to see her cat curled up in the middle of the couch. "Oh, that little booger," she rasped, stepping closer to get a good look at Max. "I'm sorry, Cole. He just ... he has no manners. And I'm to blame. I spoil him rotten."

Closing the door, Cole chuckled and motioned for her to follow him into the kitchen. "Let sleeping dogs lie. We've got a bit of work to do, and we don't need any four-legged help up on the counters."

Kari cringed with guilty embarrassment. "Has he been up on your counters too, going through your cabinets?"

Cole raised his brows. "No, not that I know of. I was just joking."

"Well, sorry to say, he does that. Just push him off if he tries it here."

Cole shook his head, then grabbed an apron for Kari. It was a lightweight gingham affair with ruffles his mother had bequeathed to him as a joke when he moved from home to start college. His mother was an excellent cook and was not afraid to insist that her boys as well as her girls learn how to cook too. He was forever grateful to her for that, and he'd developed a real appreciation – even love – for cooking. It gave him a creative outlet that was tasty to enjoy and share with others.

Kari eyed the apron, then laughed. "Where's yours?"

Grinning, Cole whipped out a crisp white cotton apron and tied it around his waist. "I'm not afraid to get my hands dirty in the kitchen, but my clothes I preferred to keep clean."

Kari laughed again. "I should have thought of that when I started my recent painting venture. I have a full-front cotton duck apron somewhere, but I was so eager to jump in and get started again, I never bothered to look for it very hard."

"Thus your spotted and streaked multi-color tee-shirt."

"Yeah."

Cole shrugged. "A different approach ... but if it works for you, who cares what your clothes end up looking like?"

After washing her hands at the sink and drying them on a paper towel, Kari turned to face Cole and rubbed her palms together. "So ... what can I do to help – that won't ruin everything?"

* * * * *

"Oh, my gosh, this is unbelievable!" Kari exclaimed as she savored her first bite of Cole's chicken portabella concoction. "If I had the money, I'd hire you as my personal chef! You really should open your own restaurant," she gushed. "Where did you learn to cook like this?" She didn't even wait for him to answer as she stabbed her plate with her fork for another bite. "I'm sorry I'm being such a pig, but this is so *good!*"

Cole laughed as he watched Kari devour her serving. "I have my mother to thank for forcing all us boys in the Jor–" He caught himself before blurting out his real last name, then quickly recovered and finished, "...all the boys in our family to learn how to cook."

The Cat's Fancy

Gwynn E. Ambrose

Swallowing her last bite, Kari looked up briefly from her plate and admitted, "My mother's a decent enough cook, but she never made anything like this. This is … this is real gourmet cooking. And poor thing, she tried and tried to teach me to cook, but I just managed the basics – you know, boiling water without walking off and letting the pot burn dry."

Cole laughed again, eyeing the lovely woman sitting across the table from him. She was pretty, funny, and a joy to be around. Why had he lied to her and kept his real identity from her? It was a spur of the moment thing, a bad decision that he regretted yet still had to deal with. But how? How could he tell her the truth now, and not ruin everything?

Kari cleaned the rest of her plate, then sat back with a sigh of satisfaction. "I'd lick the plate like Max does, but we don't do that in other people's homes." She giggled.

Cole found himself laughing yet again. When had he ever been with a woman who seemed so at ease with herself that she could poke fun at herself and not worry about seeming unattractive to the opposite sex? Maybe she wasn't worried about appearing attractive to him. Maybe she wasn't even thinking along those lines, where he was concerned. Perhaps her string of bad luck with men – men that her cat Max had managed to run off – had put her off the idea of a real relationship. He wondered…

"So, what other talents do you have, that I'll be interested in?" Kari teased.

The question caught Cole off guard for a second, but he quickly recovered. Grinning, he said, "Patience. I don't want to overwhelm you all at once with my fabulous repertoire."

With that cute, infectious giggle of hers, she got up from the table and grabbed her dishes. "Well, okay, I can wait, I guess. Since I'm a cooking klutz, I'll just do the dishes."

"Oh, no. I'll take care of things. You just go into the living room and relax."

"No," Kari insisted. "It's only fair. If you're going to feed me such wonderful food, I'll help with the cleanup."

Cole shrugged and smiled, feeling suddenly very domestic. It felt … good.

He gathered his dishes and followed her over to the sink.

CHAPTER 11

The Best Laid Plans

I sat in the living room floor, watching Kari lounge on the red couch as she talked on the phone with her friend Raschelle. She seemed very content and happy – happier than I'd seen her in a long time. This, I suspected, was due to the fact that she was pleased with her new mate, Cole.

Satisfied with my selection, I licked my left shoulder, smoothing down my fur. It had been much easier than I'd suspected it would be to find a suitable man for my human Kari. She seemed to like him, and he provided excellent leftovers for my enjoyment – admittedly the best I'd ever tasted. The chicken with mushrooms was delectable – although I'd had to help myself to it while Kari and Cole were otherwise occupied, cleaning the dishes at the sink. Cole seemed good-natured about the incident, while Kari did make quite a fuss about my jumping up on Cole's table. Oh well. One has to take matters into one's own paws, if one expects to receive what one deserves.

I licked my right front paw in memory of the delicious helping of chicken I was able to procure before they spotted me on the table. *Yes, very yummy.*

Normally I would take little interest in Kari's phone conversations, as she usually prattled on about things of no concern to me, but on this particular occasion, I decided to stick around and find out just what she thought of Cole, the man I had procured for her as a possible mate. She, of course, seemed delighted as she discussed Cole with Raschelle.

"Not only is he to die for, he can *cook!*" Kari gushed. "No, I'm not hallucinating, and no he is not gay. He mentioned a girlfriend. *Ex-girlfriend.*"

Kari giggled. "No! I'm not that kind of girl. It's only our second date."

I got up and strolled away, satisfied that things were going well. Listening to any more of this would just be a waste of time, I decided, as I heard Kari suggest, "Well, maybe you *should* check him out. You know my taste in men can't be trusted. But I'm telling you, I think he's the real deal."

Bored, I ambled over to the window behind the drapes, where I usually made my departure from the apartment for my frequent outdoor forays. To my dismay, the window was shut. I ducked out from behind the drapes and meowed loudly in disapproval. Kari was still talking with animated glee on the phone and didn't notice. I stalked off to the bedroom to sulk and perhaps find something naughty to occupy my attention, like unrolling more toilet paper, or knocking things off Kari's dresser – accidentally, of course.

* * * * *

The days spent at the Manning Baltimore office were almost tolerable as Cole occupied his free thoughts with musings of Kari. She'd showed him the modern-art-style portrait she was painting of Max. It was bold yet whimsical, a perfect portrayal of her wickedly smart pet. Cole was still amazed by her deft mastery of painting. She was much better than she gave herself credit for, and he couldn't understand why her self-confidence was so low. He toyed with the idea of contacting a couple local galleries on her behalf, but he didn't want to put her on the spot, and so he shelved that idea.

Anyway, he did have some work to do here at Manning, and he couldn't spend all his time thinking about her. But it was hard not to. Just trying to not think of her brought a smile to his face as he sorted through the personnel files on Vance' former desk.

He'd finished interviewing everyone left at Manning that Vance and Kendall hadn't managed to get rid of before he arrived. It was a short list, and he didn't like the selection that was left. Not many people who remained were worth keeping on; most of them were loyal suck-ups who'd do and say just about anything to keep their jobs. Raschelle Devreaux was an exception, and she seemed far better suited to a managerial position than the call-center. Her credentials and capabilities had been hampered at Manning by managers who refused to see her potential, and Cole was determined to rectify that situation soon.

He'd already canned Gerald Vance, the incompetent weasel, and was preparing to deal with Vice-President Robert Kendall, Vance's partner in crime in this farce of mismanagement at the Baltimore office. *What a waste of resources!*

But first he had a choice little task to take care of ... the firing of lying, underhanded Jeff Braswell. And he was going to enjoy making him squirm. He checked his watch, noting that Mr. Braswell was putting off his arrival until the very last minute. Was he nervous? Did he suspect what was coming? Cole hoped he did.

At precisely that moment, Jeff Braswell's wormy little shadow darkened the glass front of the HR VP's former office. Sitting behind Vance's desk, Cole smiled genially and motioned Braswell in. Braswell slinked in and stood waiting before the desk. "Good morning, sir. I trust everything is going well." His tone was sickeningly, obsequiously pleasant.

"Yes, exceedingly well, Mr. Braswell. Thank you for asking."

"Is there anything I can do to assist you?"

"Yes, as a matter of fact, there is."

Jeff Braswell perked hopefully, almost smiling.

"You can tell me the truth about what went on with you and Kari Ingles."

Braswell's face fell. "But ... but I have told the truth, sir."

Cole sat back in Vance's leather executive chair and studied Braswell thoughtfully. "Vance isn't here anymore to back you up. And other people I've spoken with have told a story quite different from the one you gave me the last time we talked. Would you care to amend your answer?"

"Well ... um ... I'm not sure exactly ... I mean ... um ... what do you want me to tell you?"

"The truth, Mr. Braswell. The bare, honest truth. Things will go much easier for you if you'll just come clean and tell me what really happened."

Jeff Braswell paled and swallowed with great difficulty, as if he'd suffered a sudden case of cotton-mouth. Finally he managed, "Wh-What do you want to know?"

"First of all, I'd like to know why you gave Miss Ingles such a hard time when you began your position as supervisor of the call center."

"W-Well, I didn't really ... um ... I mean ... she..."

"Yes, Mr. Braswell? She what? From what I've been able to gather, she did her best to train you to do the job she was doing temporarily until you came along and took it from her."

"Well, you see, Mr. Jordensen, Miss Ingles simply wasn't qualified–"

"With a bachelor's degree compared to your associate degree? With five years of experience in the call center, compared to your total lack of experience? In what alternate dimension would you consider yourself more qualified, Mr. Braswell?"

Before he could pretend to answer that impossible question, Cole put up a hand and gave him a condescending smile. "I know, I know. That's what you were told by your uncle and Mr. Vance. But we both know it's just a load of bull. You were hired by Vance as a favor to your uncle, and Miss Ingles was passed over for a promotion so you could take the job."

Jeff Braswell gulped but said nothing. There was nothing to

say to that accusation, because it was the truth, and both he and Cole knew it.

"So..." said Cole, sitting forward and leaning his arms on the desk. "The idea of this better-qualified woman teaching you to do the job she had been doing irked you to no end. And the very sight of her everyday made you remember that you'd sneaked in through nepotism and taken a job that should have been given to her. You didn't want her around as a constant reminder, so you thought you'd make her miserable enough to leave."

Cole straightened in his chair and eyed Braswell, who stared at the floor. "Feel free to stop and correct me if I've somehow managed to get this wrong."

Braswell said nothing, and didn't bother to look up, so Cole continued. "When she didn't pick up and leave at the first sign of trouble, you came down on her harder ... embarrassed her in front of her coworkers, and lied about her performance to cover up your own stupid mistakes. Still, she wouldn't leave. So you decided to up the ante by going to her house and hitting on her."

Braswell looked up in alarm, and Cole smiled. "Yes, I've talked with Miss Ingles. I know about everything – including her cat peeing on your tennis shoes."

Braswell's mouth opened and closed several times, like a fish lying helpless on the shore. Finally he managed, "She ... she invited me over. She–"

"Stop it!" Cole demanded, lurching forward in his chair. Braswell reared back, obviously intimidated. "I don't want to hear any more of your lame lies and excuses. At least be man enough to own up to what you did – tried to do."

"All right, all right," Braswell amended hastily. "I called her. I invited myself over to her place. I was just trying to make up for ... for ... to apologize for..."

"For being such a horse's rear?"

Braswell lowered his head.

"And no matter how altruistic that sounds, I find it hard to believe that your intention was to make amends for your previous atrocious behavior. I think you thought if she played along, you'd get a freebie, and if she didn't you'd do just what you did – set her up to take the fall in a sexual harassment complaint to get her fired."

Cole shook his head in angry amazement. "What I don't understand is how stupid Vance was to go along with it, without even raising any questions, or attempting to investigate the situation. Or ... was he in on it all along?"

Braswell sighed, deflated.

"Manning Industries should count itself lucky she hasn't filed a harassment and wrongful termination suit – *yet*."

Braswell looked up in alarm.

"Yes, that's right, you and Vance would be named as co-defendants. So you'd better hope and pray that she doesn't go ahead with it."

Cole stood up from the chair and towered behind the desk. "Now I suggest you go back to your office and clear out your things. Security is already waiting for you."

Meekly, without meeting Cole's eyes, Jeff Braswell rose from his chair and slunk out of the office.

Cole frowned, expecting that to make him feel much better than he did. It was never a good thing to have to let someone go, but in this particular case, it was a good move for the company, and the weasel deserved to lose his job for what he'd done. The bad thing was, just losing his job didn't seem nearly enough punishment for what Cole imagined he'd put Kari through in the last six months. Cole still wasn't sure he was done with Braswell yet. Maybe he'd urge Kari to file a suit for damages, even though it would mean financial loss for the company.

He shook his head, wondering how cow pies like Gerald Vance got to be in positions of authority. What idiot promoted somebody like Vance, and then allowed him to remain and do all the damage he'd done. A company that encouraged that kind of stupidity deserved to be sued for all it was worth.

The Cat's Fancy

Gwynn E. Ambrose

* * * * *

"I can't call him. I don't have his cell number," Kari said to Raschelle on the phone. "Things haven't progressed far enough for us to exchange numbers. It's just ... you know. Friendly and casual."

"But you've been having dinner at his place every night," Chelle objected. "That's more than just casual and friendly. He's *cooking* for you."

Kari thought about it and realized it was only by the grace of her wayward cat that Cole had even come to her apartment in the first place. If she hadn't left that window open...

She looked over at the window in question, hidden by drapes, and thought perhaps she ought to open it again. Max had been meowing and acting all out of sorts ever since she'd closed it. And if he couldn't get back over to Cole's apartment tonight, what guarantee did she have that Cole would come over again and invite her over?

"Hello, are you still there?" Chelle asked over the phone.

Kari returned to the present reality and realized Chelle had been saying something, but she had no idea what. "I'm sorry, I was ... um ... checking on something."

"I said," Chelle repeated, a little miffed, "you'll never guess what Hatchet Man did today."

"What?"

"He canned Braswell!"

"You're kidding!"

"No, and that's not the half of it. I think VP Kendall's next."

"Well, after Vance, I kind of expected that."

"Yeah, but here's the best part. He called me into his office and offered me a management position. Can you believe that?"

"Really?" Kari turned from the window and hugged her phone to her face with renewed interest. "What position?"

"He didn't say. He just said that my 'talents' – ha! My talents weren't being properly utilized."

Kari frowned. "He wasn't coming on to you, was he?"

"No! Are you kidding?"

"No, I'm not kidding, Chelle. You're a very intelligent and beautiful woman. And he's right about one thing, your talents are being under-utilized. You could do so much more than you have been. Manning's just been holding you back."

"Don't I know it."

"So ... when did he say this managerial position would materialize?"

"He didn't, but he told me to be patient, and when the dust settled, my loyalty to the company would be aptly rewarded."

"That's ... that's so great, Chelle. I'm really happy for you!"

There was a pause over the phone, then Chelle said, "I know that news probably doesn't make you feel so good, considering you lost your job and–"

"Oh, don't be ridiculous, Chelle. I *am* happy for you. You deserve to be promoted. Haven't I been telling you that for years?"

"Yes, but–"

"Don't worry about me. Just because Hatchet Man didn't get there in time to save my job doesn't mean I wouldn't have lost it anyway."

"Well, I'm not so sure about that. But I just had to tell somebody, even though he told me to keep it quiet until things settled down."

"I hope that doesn't take too long. Manning's in a mess. Is he actually fixing things, or just making them worse?"

"He got rid of Braswell. It can only get better after that!"

Kari laughed, feeling oddly empty and left out, now that she wasn't part of the employed population segment. She didn't belong at Manning anymore, and apparently she didn't belong anywhere. Her job search had been disappointing so far.

The Cat's Fancy　　　　　　　　Gwynn E. Ambrose

"Say, you never did tell me dreamboat's name."

"What? Oh. Oh, yeah. Cole. Um ... Daniel Cole."

"Daniel?" Chelle echoed suspiciously.

"Yeah. Why? Is there something wrong with that name?"

"No, no. It's just that the new guy here at work, you know, Hatchet Man, has the same first name. Daniel Jordensen."

"Well, I'm sure a lot of guys are named Daniel, Chelle. It's not that big a coincidence."

"No ... I guess not. But still. It's kind of ... weird."

"No it's not. Daniel's a perfectly normal name."

"No, I didn't mean the name is weird. It's the fact that ... you know ... Daniel Cole shows up at your apartment complex the same time Daniel Jordensen shows up here at Manning. And your Daniel – Cole – is real cagey about what he does for a living, and says it's just temporary. And didn't you say he was a real looker, with dark wavy hair, and big brown eyes?"

"Well, yeah ... but that could describe lots of guys." Kari frowned as she looked at her neglected living room window again, the one she kept ensconced in heavy drapes. Why had she chosen to keep that window covered all the time, when the larger windows and the sliding glass doors were allowed to dispense daylight? She couldn't remember now what the reason was, and it seemed kind of weird. About as weird as Chelle's idea that Cole could be Manning Industries' Hatchet Man. There was no way ... no way. Cole was too sweet to be a coldblooded corporate executioner, going from district office to district office to gather, cull, and fire people. A man who did that for a living ... how could he live with himself? He would have to be soulless, uncaring demon. And Cole certainly didn't fit that description.

Cole had seemed supportive and nonjudgmental when she told him about her altercation with Jeff Braswell and losing her job because of it. Cole kindly congratulated her when her appointment with the Employment Office went surprisingly well. In fact, he was quick to tell her he was sure things would go well ... as if he had some kind of inside knowledge.

90

Someone with pull and authority had canceled Manning's denial of her benefits with just a simple phone call. Who could it have been? Nobody at Manning with that kind of pull would have given a flip about her. But the Hatchet Man had promised Chelle he'd look into things. Had he actually called on her behalf? And if Cole seemed to know it was going to happen...

No. There was no way the two Daniels were one and the same. She refused to entertain the idea any further.

"Just invite me over," Chelle was saying on the phone, "and make sure he's there. I want to meet this wonder man of yours. Any guy that'll wear an apron and cook dinner – I've got to see for myself!"

Kari managed to laugh at Chelle's upbeat insistence. "I'll do what I can, but no guarantees."

Kari said goodbye and ended the call, but frowned as she set aside the phone. How *would* she manage to slip Chelle into the conversation and get her invited over to Cole's place for dinner?

She eyed Max, pacing around and meowing, disturbed because she wouldn't let him out. It was getting late, about the time Cole usually came home from work. She went over to Max. Smiling deviously, she offered, "You wanna go outside, baby?"

Max meowed loudly and scrambled over to the patio doors.

"Good boy," Kari encouraged. "Go get Cole."

CHAPTER 12

Cat's Out of the Bag

"There you are, right on time," Cole said as he opened his patio doors for Max. Max came slinking in and ambled toward the kitchen with the swagger of a well-fed cat expecting more of the same treatment.

"I've already set out your pre-dinner snack, just the way you like it," Cole said as he headed toward the bedroom to change clothes. When Max tossed him an offhanded meow, he added, "Oh, and stay off the table." Max ignored him and disappeared around the corner into the kitchen.

"Not that there's anything edible on the table," Cole mumbled as he loosened his tie and walked into the bedroom. "It's the principle. Food on the table, feet – and paws – on the floor."

* * * * *

A few minutes after he'd changed his clothes, Cole heard a knock on his apartment door, right on cue. He smiled and let Kari into the living room.

"Oh, there you are, you naughty Maxi-kitty," she gushed, giggling apologetically as she headed toward the comfy couch where Max lay ensconced on his throne. She turned to Cole, not making much of an attempt to grab up her cat. "I was out on the patio earlier today, and–"

"–you forgot to close the doors." Cole waved a hand dismissively in the air. "Happens to me all the time. That's how

Max keeps getting in here."

Kari stood staring at him and giggled again. He knew she was waiting for the usual invitation to stay for dinner. He smiled. "London broil?"

"Sounds yummy." She sniffed the air. "And smells yummy too!"

"Dinner'll be ready in just a little while. Let me go check on the roasted potatoes."

"Um ... can I help with something?" she offered brightly.

He shook his head. "Everything's all taken care of."

"I'm ... uh ... going to powder my nose."

"Sure. Just keep your shoes on."

She gave him a look and then remembered her warning to him the other day about Max. She busted out laughing and scurried down the short hallway to the bathroom.

* * * * *

Once inside the bathroom, Kari pulled her cell phone out of her jeans pocket and dialed Chelle's number. When Chelle answered, Kari whispered, barely able to contain her excitement, "Call me in about five minutes and say you're at my apartment. I'll go get you. I'm sure Cole won't mind if I bring you over. He always makes extra food."

Already in the parking lot, Chelle agreed, and Kari ended the call, placing her phone back in her pocket. Fluffing her hair and checking her barely-there makeup in the mirror, Kari headed for the door, and then remembered to flush the toilet to keep up her pretense.

She hated sneaking around to pull a fast one on Cole, but she did want to show him off to Chelle and have him meet her best friend.

* * * * *

93

The Cat's Fancy

Gwynn E. Ambrose

"This is fabulous – so tender!" Kari complimented. "And the potatoes are to die for. What did you put on them?"

"What about the broccoli?" Cole teased. "It's going to feel left out."

She giggled and squirmed in her seat, barely able to sit still. She expected her phone to ring at any second, and she was having trouble concentrating on anything long enough to pretend everything was normal and she wasn't up to something.

Just when she forced herself to relax, her phone chirped and startled her. "Oh, I'm sorry," she exclaimed. "I was expecting a call, so I brought my cell phone with me. I'll take it in the other room."

Cole smiled as he watched her get up from the table. He was totally oblivious to her scheme to introduce him to Chelle – or he was a great actor and was just pretending to be oblivious. Either way, he seemed totally unconcerned by her erratic and jumpy behavior. She didn't normally giggle at everything. Or ... did she?

She scurried into the living room and answered her cell. Talking loud enough to make sure Cole overheard, she said, "Oh, sure. I'll be there in a minute. Bye." She ducked her head into the kitchen. "That was my girlfriend. She stopped by and is waiting at my apartment."

Cole suddenly looked stricken.

"I-I'm sorry. I don't mean to interrupt the fabulous dinner you cooked, but I can't let Chelle stand out in the hallway, can I?"

"Chelle? Raschelle?" Cole echoed.

"Uh ... yeah." Kari frowned, wondering why Cole looked so green around the gills. She didn't remember mentioning Raschelle to him, but maybe she had when she'd told him about her experience at Manning. She shrugged and said, "I'll be right back. I want you to meet her. You don't mind if I bring her over for a minute, do you?"

"Sure..." Cole whispered, as if he were out of breath.

Kari smiled and darted out of the apartment, leaving the door cracked so she could get back in.

She saw Chelle coming down the hallway toward her. Regally tall, she looked elegant even in jeans. Of course she didn't wear ratty tennis shoes, she wore stylish flats that made her look all neat and put together. Next to her, Kari felt like a short slob.

When Kari ducked her head back into Cole's living room and called out to announce her return, she didn't hear or see him. Only Max responded, waking up and meowing softly as he stretched out on Cole's couch.

"I see the little varmint has made himself at home here," Chelle announced with a note of wary disdain in her voice.

Kari ignored Chelle's discomfort around Max and motioned her forward. "Come on, I think Cole's still in the kitchen."

"Mmm," Chelle said, "something smells good!"

Kari giggled. "I know. Isn't it amazing? He really *can* cook, and it's *edible* too!"

When Kari rounded the corner and entered the kitchen with Chelle in tow, she found Cole standing at the table, putting out another place setting. He looked up with just a hint of tension on his face. She felt bad putting him on the spot and interrupting their dinner time, but introducing him to Chelle was very important to her, and she was sure he'd understand that.

"Cole, this is Chelle – Raschelle Devreaux. Chelle, Cole – Daniel Cole."

Kari watched an even smile form on Cole's face as he moved forward and held out his hand. "Pleased to meet you, Chelle."

Kari turned just in time to see an odd look of surprise on Chelle's face. With raised browse, she shook Cole's hand. "Likewise, *Cole*. Kari's told me so much about you, I feel like we've already met."

Cole gave Chelle a look that seemed almost wary, then

THE CAT'S FANCY GWYNN E. AMBROSE

laughed softly, with just a second's hesitation.

Kari frowned. Both Cole and Chelle were acting a bit odd, almost as if they were uncomfortable around each other. But then she decided it was her imagination, because immediately Cole invited Chelle to sit down and have dinner with them, even though they'd already started. Chelle begged off, saying she didn't want to interrupt and really should be going, but Cole was very persistent, and even went so far as to say his feelings would be hurt if Chelle skipped out. Finally Chelle relented, and Kari could feel the tension in the room ease a bit. Still it was strange how they acted around each other, as if they already knew one another. But that couldn't be...

"Oh my, this looks really good," Chelle commented as she dished food onto her plate. "And you cooked this yourself?"

Cole smiled pleasantly. "Kari offered to help, but I wouldn't let her."

"Smart move."

"Hey!" Kari objected, feeling a bit put out by the veiled insult.

Chelle laughed, then took a bite of the London broil. Closing her eyes, she chewed slowly and swallowed, then announced, "Mr. Cole, you are a culinary god!"

Kari and Cole laughed, and Kari could feel the earlier tension slipping away. Or had she just imagined it was there to begin with?

"So, you just arrived in Baltimore?" Chelle prodded as she dug into her dinner.

"Yes," Cole admitted. "And you're a native?"

"New York, actually."

Cole perked his brows and nodded. "How did you end up here?"

"An ex-husband."

This time it was Kari's eyebrows that went up. "I didn't know you were married."

Chelle shrugged, the filmy outer layer of her silky blouse

96

shimmering with the movement. "I don't like to talk about it. Devon was ... well ... a part of my life best forgotten."

"So, is Devreaux your maiden name or—"

"Yes," Chelle said decisively. "There was no way I was going to go through life with that lying snake's last name after we split." Chelle glared pointedly at Cole and added, "Men who lie should, in my opinion, be shot. It would save the world a lot of heartache."

Startled by Chelle's venomous tone, Kari blinked and glanced at Cole, whose even smile and glittering dark eyes seemed to throw a silent challenge in Chelle's direction.

"Um ... wow, Cole, you've outdone yourself again," Kari announced, trying to change the subject. "Again, dinner was fabulous."

Cole turned his attention to her, and his expression softened. "Tonight, though, we'll put the leftovers away immediately, to keep you-know-who from helping himself to whatever's sitting on the table."

Kari cringed and grimaced with guilt. "I know Max is a naughty kitty, but—"

"Naughty kitty?" Chelle piped, obviously over her earlier ill-humor. "He's a menace to society, that's what he is."

"Now, Chelle," Kari chastised. "He *likes* you."

"How can you tell, in between the yowls and the shredding of his claws? Good grief, I'd hate to think what he'd do to me if he *didn't* like me."

Kari shook her head. "It was just those silky pants of yours. He couldn't resist. That's why I don't wear nylons."

"They're out of fashion anyway. Tights in the winter — that's the only acceptable alternative."

"Well," said Cole, rising from his chair, "as fascinating as this fashionista talk about leg-wear is, I need to get the kitchen cleaned up. Why don't you ladies retire to the living room, and I'll bring us all some after-dinner coffee?"

"Oh, let me help with that," Kari insisted. "I can at least

clean up."

"No, no," Cole said, shooing her out of the kitchen. "You two go relax, and I'll be there in a bit."

Kari looked at Chelle and shrugged. "Okay, if you're sure."

"Absolutely."

"Thank you for dinner, Cole," Chelle said. "I appreciate your making room at the table for me, considering I just popped in unannounced."

"No problem. I'm glad you were able to join us."

* * * * *

"So, what do you think of him?" Kari whispered to Chelle as she hoisted Max up into her arms to make room for them to sit on the couch. Max wriggled and jumped down, obviously incensed by her audacity in disturbing his evening nap. He stalked away and sat down on the living room carpet to watch them.

"Oh, he's dreamy, all right," Chelle admitted. "And he *can* cook. No doubt about it."

"Isn't he just perfect?" Kari gushed, touching a hand to Chelle's arm.

"Honey, you don't know a thing about him ... where he's from, where he's been, what he does for a living. You need to get to know him better before you go all head-over-heels about him."

Kari tilted her head and stared at Chelle in dismay. "You don't like him?"

"I didn't say that. He's gorgeous, charming, and entertaining. And he's definitely got charisma. But, girlfriend, he's a stranger. You've known him less than a week. You need to hold your horses and not get ahead of yourself."

Kari huddled down on the cushy couch. "I can't help it, Chelle. He's the first guy I've felt this way about in ... I don't know when. It's like I instantly liked him the minute I saw him. I don't know what it is–"

"Couldn't be indigestion, could it? You've been eating some mighty rich cooking lately."

Kari reprimanded Chelle with a little slap on her shoulder "I'm serious. He's ... he's so ... I don't know what it is about him, but–"

"Ready for coffee, ladies?" Cole announced, carrying a new black lacquer serving tray with three steaming cups, a small pitcher of milk, and a crystal bowl sporting various sweetener packets. He set the tray down on the coffee table and then sat in the matching oversized chair facing the couch.

"I could get used to service like this," Chelle admitted. "Are you sure you aren't a butler by trade?"

Cole chuckled. "No. Just occasionally – on the side."

Kari, still unsettled by Chelle's reticence regarding Cole, tried to get into a more pleasant mood, but her worry wouldn't leave entirely. Max approved of Cole, obviously, but Chelle seemed to have some reservations she wasn't at liberty to discuss as long as Cole was in the room. Once they left Cole's apartment, Kari intended to have a serious talk with her.

Kari put milk and sugar in her cup and took a sip. It was the best coffee she'd had in ... well, it was the best coffee she'd ever had. "What kind of blend is this? It's wonderful." How was it that everything Cole touched seemed to be perfect – better than perfect? Or was it just her imagination?

Chelle tasted her coffee and pressed her lips together. "Mmmm, good stuff."

"Cole said he would like to open his own restaurant someday," Kari announced. "Isn't that right?" she said, looking over at Cole expectantly for confirmation.

Before he could answer, Chelle piped up, "What's stopping you? You should have your own restaurant already."

Cole shrugged. "Other obligations. Timing. Sometimes you can't always do what you want, when you want."

Chelle nodded knowingly, as if she shared some secret understanding with him. Kari frowned, wondering about it. The

The Cat's Fancy

Gwynn E. Ambrose

two of them seemed to have a special bond that somehow didn't include her, and she felt left out, almost jealous.

Trying to reign in her suspicions, she took another sip of coffee, then glanced around, looking for Max. When she didn't see him anywhere, she instantly went into panic mode. "Uh-oh. Did anyone see where Max went?" She set her cup down on the saucer with a clatter and put it on the coffee table.

"Don't worry," Cole said, putting up a hand to calm her. "I'm sure he's fine."

"But he's liable to get into–"

"Don't worry about it, Kari. There's nothing in this apartment that's dear to me, that can't be replaced if it gets–"

"Shredded," Chelle clarified. "Like it's been run through a wood-chipper. That beast has claws like a grizzly bear."

Cole laughed. "He seems harmless enough."

"You'll see when he rakes his claws down your leg and slices up your pants."

"He was just ... *admiring* your slacks, Chelle," Kari offered lamely.

"Yeah, like he was going to go out and get a pair for himself. Um-hm."

Worried and guilty, Kari started to get up from the couch to go look for her cat, but Cole shot up and said, "I'll go find him. I'm sure he's just gone somewhere to find a quiet place to finish his nap."

As soon as Cole headed down the hallway toward his bedroom to look for Max, Kari whispered to Chelle, "What's up with you and Cole? It's like you ... you know something about him that I don't. Don't you like him?"

Chelle sighed. "Honey, he's everything you said he was ... and *more*." Glancing at the hallway, she saw him returning with Max in his arms and added under her breath, "And any man who can put up with that cat of yours and keep smiling has got to be special. Just make sure you get to know him a little better. That's all I'm saying."

100

"Oh, I intend to."

* * * * *

As Kari gathered up Max and thanked Cole again for dinner and coffee, Chelle reached for the tray on the coffee table and proceeded to carry it into the kitchen. "I'll catch up to you, Kari. The least I can do for that fabulous dinner I enjoyed is carry this back into the kitchen for the chef."

With Max squirming in her arms, Kari didn't seem eager to argue. "Okay, see you in a sec. And thanks again, Cole. Really."

"My pleasure, Kari. See you later."

Cole watched Kari leave and close the apartment door behind her. Then he turned on Raschelle, standing in the living room holding the coffee serving tray. Obviously she was looking for an opportunity to speak with him alone. He took the tray from her. "Thanks for not outing me to Kari."

"Oh, don't think for a second I did you a favor, *Cole Jordensen*. What is Cole anyway, your middle name?"

He nodded. "My mother's maiden name."

Raschelle shook her head, clearly disappointed by the whole mess he'd created. He carried the tray into the kitchen and set it down on the counter, with Raschelle following close behind. When he turned to face her, he found her steaming with anger accentuated by her big coppery hair and flaming red fingernails. She was quite a package, and he dreaded tangling with her – especially now that she had something on him that she could use to get the better of him. "Look, it's not what you think," he said.

"Oh, then what is it, *Mr. Cole?*"

He scowled. "That was ... I got caught by surprise. I didn't think things through. When I ran into Kari and realized who she was, I didn't want her to know that I worked at Manning Industries. So ... I fudged on my real name. It was a mistake. I know that now. But at the time..."

Raschelle shook her mountain of hair. "What are you even

doing here, living in her apartment complex?"

"That was a coincidence. Honestly, I didn't plan it. I found the month-by-month rental listing online and figured it would be better than staying in an executive hotel. I hate kitchenettes that don't have a full-size oven. And it wasn't that much more expensive – except for the rental furniture. I didn't even know about Kari when I moved in here. Besides, I wasn't planning on staying here that long, because–"

"Because in a couple weeks, you're going to be moving on, when you're done cleaning up Manning's Baltimore office."

Cole shrugged. What could he say?

Raschelle paced over and poked him in the chest with her hard, pointy index finger with its flame-red nail. He backed up against the counter as she growled, "Kari's my best friend, and I don't want to see her hurt."

"I don't either. I–"

"She really cares about you. She *likes* you. What are you gonna do about *that*, Mr. Cole?"

He let out a ragged breath. "I ... I don't know."

"You don't know! What is this, some kind of cute little game you're playing?"

"No."

"Don't you care about her feelings at all?"

"I..." He lowered his gaze. "Yes, I care."

Raschelle snorted, and he looked her straight in the eyes. She gave him a hard, scrutinizing stare, then stepped back and said, "Well, this is your mess. You clean it up. And you better do it quick. She deserves to know the truth. You can't keep lying to her, even if you *are* leaving in a week or two."

"So ... you're not going to rat on me?"

Raschelle tossed her head back regally and looked down her nose at him. "I don't like keeping secrets from friends, but I'll stay quiet about this as long as you promise to come clean. *Soon.*"

* * * * *

When Chelle arrived at the apartment a minute or two later, Kari had already started wondering why she'd stayed behind at Cole's apartment using that flimsy excuse of helping to clean up the after-dinner coffee dishes. Clearly she'd wanted time alone with Cole – but why?

"Gotta go," Chelle said. "Work tomorrow. Night, girlfriend." She reached out and gave Kari one of her usual hugs, but it seemed too quick, like she was in a hurry to leave.

"What's going on, Chelle? What is it with Cole? There's ... is something going on you're not telling me?"

"What in the world are you talking about, girl? You just keep a tight rein on that man. He's too fine to be runnin' loose. Now, I gotta go, for real. It was fun. I'll call ya later. Bye now."

Before Kari could stop her, Chelle was out the door, pulling it shut behind her. Kari shook her head, puzzled by Chelle's peculiar behavior. It wasn't like her to avoid anything, and she was definitely dodging the subject of Cole. Obviously Chelle knew *something* she wasn't telling. What could it be?

Kari pace aimlessly, then turned off the lights and headed for her bedroom. Max was already sprawled out in the middle of the bed, snoozing soundly. Kari put on her pajamas and brushed her teeth, but still she couldn't settle down to go to sleep. Chelle's bizarre behavior when she'd seen Cole left Kari restless and worried. Was she imagining things, or was Chelle holding back some sort of information about Cole? And if she was, how had she found it out, and why wouldn't she tell her?

Standing in the dark by the bed, Kari fluffed her hair irritably. She stepped away from the bed, but had nowhere to go in the dark. *I have to get to the bottom of this, or it's going to drive me nuts! Chelle was so eager to meet Cole ... then she couldn't seem to get away fast enough. And what was the deal with her staying behind at his apartment? She obviously wanted to talk to him alone, without me around. Does she know him from somewhere? Oh, my gosh! Have they dated before? No, no. He*

THE CAT'S FANCY

GWYNN E. AMBROSE

just got into Baltimore. How could Chelle possibly know him?

Sighing miserably, Kari knew the only way she'd get answers to her worries and questions was to make Chelle tell her what was going on. *I'll invite her to lunch, pick her up at work, and take her somewhere nice, close by, so she can't use her lunch hour limit as an excuse to rush back to work and avoid telling me everything. Somehow I'll get her to talk.*

With that decision made, Kari finally relaxed enough to settle into bed. It still took her more than an hour of tossing and turning to finally drop off to sleep. Once she did sleep, she dreamed of Cole ... dreamed that she kept trying to reach him, but he was always out of range. And the harder she tried, the farther away he got, until he was so far away, he disappeared altogether.

* * * * *

At 11:50, Kari sat in her car parked in a visitor spot in the Manning Industries parking lot. She never thought she'd see this place again – not that she wanted to. But today she was on a mission: to make Chelle spill about Cole.

She checked her watch again and reached for her phone to see if Chelle was on her way down. About that time, she saw the employee entrance door at the side of the building swing open and expected to see Chelle. Instead ... instead she saw a tall man, muscularly fit and well-dressed in a charcoal suit, emerge and head for the parking spots reserved for Manning executives. She did a double-take and squinted, trying to see his face better. He had wavy dark hair, just like – *no, it couldn't be! Could it? No.*

He walked with smooth confidence and used his key fob to unlock the doors of a silver BMW with a black convertible top. Opening the driver's door, he slid into the car.

Kari jumped with a start as the passenger door of her car opened. Chelle slid into the seat beside her, all smiles, and asked, "Ready to go?" When Kari didn't answer, she asked, "What are you looking at?"

"That man!" Kari pointed at the silver BMW backing out of the parking space some distance away.

"What man?"

"In that car! That convertible. Who is he?"

Chelle shrugged. "How should I know? I don't pay attention to who drives what – unless somebody tries to run me over."

"But ... but..." Kari sighed helplessly. "He looked just like Cole. I'd swear he was Cole!"

"Really," Chelle said with a deadpan stare. She didn't say anything else for a few seconds, then laughed softly. "Sounds like you got Cole on the brain, girlfriend."

Kari's mind raced as she tried to think straight. *How could that man possibly be Cole? No way could he be Cole!* But then she remembered. She turned on Chelle. "Didn't you tell me a couple days ago that Hatchet Man had the same first name as Cole? And when you described what he looked like, he sounded just like Cole!" She narrowed her eyes, scrutinizing Chelle for any sign of weakness, but Chelle just sat there like a statue. "He *is* Cole, isn't he? Cole is Hatchet Man!"

Chelle frowned. "Look, I don't know what's going on. I–"

"Oh my gosh, oh my gosh!" Kari put her hands on her cheeks that were suddenly flushed. "Why did he ... what is he doing, living down the hall from me? Why did he *lie* to me?"

Chelle grabbed her shoulders and turned her around to face her. "Listen to me. I recognized him from work when I came over last night, but I didn't want to say anything until I had a chance to talk to him and find out what was going on. I don't think he meant to ... well, I don't think he was trying to pull anything over on you, Kari. He just happened to find the apartment in your building online. It was advertised for monthly lease. I guess he didn't want to stay in a hotel. Something about a full-size oven.

"Anyway, I'm not getting into the middle of this. You're going to have to talk to him yourself to find out what's going on. Now, can we please go to lunch? I'm on a limited schedule. Paul

THE CAT'S FANCY

Gwynn E. Ambrose

and Alicia said they'd cover for me if I came back a little late, but I don't want to cut into their lunchtime, so let's go. Okay?"

Jittery from the reality that had been dumped on her, Kari swiped a hand across her teary eyes and fumbled with the key in the ignition.

"You want me to drive?" Chelle offered. "My car's right over there."

Kari let out deflated sigh. "Yeah, sure."

They got out of her car and went to Chelle's late-model Volvo. With another sigh, Kari said, "I'm sorry if I seemed like I was jumping all over you. I know this isn't your problem. And, to tell you the truth, I don't think I'm going to be fit company for lunch."

"You want to make it another time, then?" Chelle offered charitably.

Kari shrugged. She didn't have much of an appetite anymore, but she couldn't ruin Chelle's lunch hour because of it. This situation wasn't Chelle's fault. "No, I'll be okay. I just ... I'm a little confused about everything."

She just wished Chelle had told her up front about Cole, instead of covering for him. Of course, when she thought back on things, she remembered it was Chelle who'd warned her to take it easy with Cole. It was Chelle who'd initially been suspicious of Cole's possible dual identity. And poor Chelle walked right into the middle of Cole's little scam when she'd popped over last night to check him out for Kari. Chelle obviously did the best she could, trying to spare Kari the embarrassment of learning the truth about Cole until she could find out herself what he was up to.

As Chelle drove them to a local eatery they'd both frequented when Kari was still working at Manning, Kari's mind pitched and rolled over the waves created by this situation with Cole. The thing that bothered – worried – her was that Cole had lied to her about who he really was. Had he been ashamed to admit that he worked for the same company that had done her wrong? Or was he trying some sneaky, underhanded method of finding out about her and what had happened with her termination, so he could use that inside information against her to protect Manning and the dirtbags who'd been responsible for taking her job from her?

No. He'd apparently done just the opposite. She realized now he was most likely the one responsible for making sure she got her unemployment compensation after some high-level bum at Manning had denied it – most likely Vance. And then he'd fired Vance, and Braswell too.

Still ... how could she face him now ... now that she knew he'd been lying to her the whole time, pretending to be someone else? That whole thing creeped her out. And to think she'd been ready to fall for him in a big way...

Maybe that was it. Maybe because he was working for Manning and knew he'd be leaving after his assignment was done ... maybe he thought it would be easier if he just pretended to be someone he wasn't. Then, when he left, it would be like she'd had a nice time with a nice guy, and could let it go because she knew it would end, and it was over. Maybe he was trying to not get involved.

But to avoid getting involved, wouldn't that mean he thought there was a chance he would *want* to get involved? She shook her head and pressed her hands to the top of her skull to keep her brain from exploding.

"Okay," Chelle said as she brought the car to stop in a parking space at the eatery. She turned the car off, unbuckled her seatbelt, and turned to face Kari. "Here are the ground rules. You can talk about anything you want to during lunch – even your evil cat. But you cannot discuss you-know-who, because I don't know what's going on, and I don't want to get into the middle of this thing between you and you-know-who. Okay?"

Kari nodded.

"Alrighty then ... let's go have a nice, relaxing lunch."

The Cat's Fancy

* * * * *

When Kari and Chelle returned to Manning's parking lot, the silver convertible was still gone. Relieved yet disappointed, Kari left but didn't go straight home. On a whim, she drove around until she ended up in her old college stomping grounds. She had enjoyed living in the area surrounding the city campus, with its older apartment buildings and stores converted to specialty shops catering to the elite educated crowd and the student population. It was an atmosphere that offered a sense of belonging to a community, and she missed that. The Garden Plaza Apartment complex was nice enough, but it didn't have the eclectic amenities that a college area steeped in art and literature and the culture of higher learning could offer.

As Kari trolled down the narrow double-parked street lined on both sides with shops frequented by students and upscale socialites, she felt a sense of déjà vu – and loss. She wanted to stop, find a parking place, and spend a couple worthless hours in a quaint coffee shop, absorbing the ambiance of the young and carefree. It was a tempting thought.

And then she saw it – the old three-story brick building that had once housed a caning operation. The time she'd gone inside several years ago, the building's storefront had been converted to a gift and rummage shop. That shop was long-gone, and the building was now closed and for sale. She had remembered immediately loving the high ceiling and ambient light of the building's interior. It was an old structure, but it had a charm that couldn't be bought, stolen, or imitated by a new building. She remembered thinking what a perfect art gallery it would make, and–

The impatient honking of a car horn behind her woke Kari from her daydreaming. She eyed the green light suspended above and urged her car ahead as she stole one last longing glance at the vacant building for sale. But who was she kidding? She didn't have the money to buy it, and she certainly couldn't get a loan, being unemployed. Returning her attention to her driving, she decided it was time to stop dreaming and go home to face reality.

* * * * *

Cole knew something was up the second Raschelle Devreaux charged into his office. She showed up almost immediately after he'd returned from lunch, as if she'd been waiting for him. He suspected Lori, the receptionist at the front lobby, had called Raschelle as soon as she'd learned he was back in his office.

Cole tried to smile pleasantly as he offered, "Have a seat, Raschelle. What's on your—"

"Skip the pleasantries, Mr. Jordensen. Cat's out of the bag. Kari saw you get into your convertible at lunchtime today."

Cole felt his smile fall like an avalanche. "So ... what did she say?"

With her hands propped on her hips, Raschelle glared down on him. "You can bet your buttery biscuits, she wasn't too happy with you. And I'm not too happy either, getting caught in the middle of this. I told you to be quick about straightening things out with her. And now look what's gone and happened."

Cole put up his hands in dismay. "I didn't even get a chance to talk to her."

"Yeah, well, it's a little late for talk. I don't know what you're going to do about this, but you better fix things somehow – that's all I got to say, mister."

With that, Raschelle turned and stormed out of the office, leaving Cole wondering how bad the collateral damage really was, and whether or not he *could* fix things with Kari.

CHAPTER 13

Truth and Consequences

"No, Max, you're not going out on the patio today," Kari insisted.

Max meowed loudly and scratched at the vertical blinds covering the double glass doors leading to the small balcony outside.

"Stop it!" Kari hollered, charging toward him. "I told you *no*. You're not going over there!"

Max yowled and pounced on her feet, digging his claws into the tender skin next to the straps of her sandals.

"Ouch! Cut it out!" Kari pulled one foot and then the other out of Max's grasp. He got up and batted her legs with his front paws, then stalked away from her, yowling again as he headed for the bedroom.

"Bad kitty!" she yelled after him. "Very bad kitty! What has gotten into you?"

She turned and looked at the patio doors, mumbling to herself, "You just don't understand. I can't have you going over there anymore. I'm not having anything to do with that man from now on – not after he lied to me and made a complete fool of me!"

She turned back toward the bedroom to find Max had ignored her and disappeared. He was mad at her, and she understood why, but unfortunately she couldn't make him understand why she couldn't let him do what he wanted. It simply wasn't something she could allow – him going over to Daniel Cole Jordensen's apartment and making himself at home. Not anymore. Cole Jordensen, the lying sneak, was off-limits to her, and to Max. Feeling the onset of tears, she swiped a hand over her eyes and plopped down on her couch. "I will not shed a tear over him. Not one!" She turned on the TV to drown out her anger and pain with the noise and ridiculousness of talk show mindless pabulum.

* * * * *

It was near dark, and when Max hadn't showed up at his patio doors, Cole got the hint the cat wouldn't show up at all tonight. Dialing Kari's apartment number, Cole didn't feel the least bit guilty getting it from her personnel file at Manning, to use for his own personal purposes. She didn't answer, so when he heard the beep to leave a message, he said, "Kari, this is Cole. We need to talk. I owe you an explanation and an apology. Please give me the opportunity to at least tell you why I did what I did. I want to tell you in person." He left his cell number and waited, but didn't expect to hear anything from her. He called her cell phone too, and left a similar message when she didn't answer.

He could understand how she'd be confused and angry over what he'd done. He was a bit confused and angry with himself for doing it. It was stupid, just something he'd done on the spur of the moment. And it wasn't really that big a deal – was it? Just because he'd lied about his name and didn't tell her he was working with Manning Industries didn't mean he was deliberately trying to hide something from her – did it?

He shook his head and headed for the kitchen to make a sandwich. Who was he trying to fool? Of course it meant he was trying to hide something from her – *the truth.*

But it was just a little thing. His last name. And his employer. Two little things. Maybe he'd give her a day or two to cool off. At least she knew he wanted to make amends. Now it was up to her to accept his apology – if she decided to allow him to offer it.

THE CAT'S FANCY

GWYNN E. AMBROSE

* * * * *

Kari threw herself into painting and ended up having to buy more pre-stretched canvases, as many as her reduced budget would allow. Painting had suddenly become a fanatical therapy substitute, allowing her to focus on creating rather than stewing in hurt and silence over the perceived wrongs that had been inflicted upon her.

Her painting room quickly became cluttered, leaving no real work space, so she was forced to stack her finished paintings in the living room along the wall beside the television. She'd gone on a cat-painting frenzy, using Max as her subject in almost every composition she completed. She'd run the gambit from impressionistic to realistic to modernistic, and had ended up with a collection of paintings she had no idea what to do with. She'd just been painting to keep her mind off Cole, and in the past week had slept little, spending most of her waking hours at her easel, slapping paint on canvases. It was the only physical and mental therapy she would allow herself – becoming the mad hermit cat-painting lady.

Meanwhile, she let Max outside in the mornings, when he demanded his freedom, but she absolutely would not let him outside in the afternoon, near the time she knew Cole would be returning to his apartment. After about the fifth day of this, Max stopped demanding that she let him out on the balcony in the early evening. He also stopped sleeping with her and stopped following her around in his usual bored-kitty way. He'd gone off to find his own methods of self-entertainment, and these included shredding her toilet paper, scattering anything she might leave on the kitchen counters, and knocking off anything that might happen to be sitting on a table or dresser or other flat surface she normally used to store personal items. In short terms, he was becoming quite the house pest. This, she knew, was all part of his way of showing his displeasure with her decision to excise Cole

Jordensen from their life.

During her week of withdrawal from Cole, Kari also vaguely noticed that Chelle was giving her space and time to come to terms with the heartache and betrayal she'd suffered. Chelle hadn't called once, nor had she offered to drop by and console her or discuss the situation with her. Kari found this to be quite odd behavior for Chelle, but she understood why she'd adopted this approach. Chelle had unwittingly been caught in the middle of Cole's scam, being in the position of knowing too much and not wanting to say anything about it. This had put Chelle in a peculiar spot of difficulty, and she probably felt it was best to keep her distance until everything blew over.

Kari decided that she'd give Chelle a call on the weekend and try to smooth things over with her. She didn't want her friendship with Chelle to be marred in any way by the underhanded antics of Cole Jordensen.

* * * * *

The call Cole had been expecting – and dreading – came at 2:30 on Friday. A new vice president had been selected to replace Robert Kendall at the Baltimore division. Obviously someone who'd reached his level of incompetency was being pigeonholed where it was hoped he'd do minimal damage until his early retirement with golden parachute benefits. This meant Cole's time in Baltimore was fast drawing to a close. And no mention had been made regarding his next assignment.

Cole hung up the phone, knowing Manning's top management would wait until the very last minute to decide what to do with him next. Perhaps they'd already decided and were waiting until the last minute to let him know his services were no longer required. They certainly wouldn't tell him their decision until they were sure they'd milked him for all the effort he was worth. That way they'd get the best mileage out of him before he bailed on them. He wished he had an alternative to consider, something else to do with his career, so he *could* bail on Manning before they told him to hit the road. His job at Manning dangled like a lynching victim swaying from a tree, and he knew his working days with the company were numbered.

He sat back in his chair, recalling how thoroughly he had enjoyed cooking for Kari, and how she'd casually mentioned to him opening his own restaurant. The offhand encouragement had started him thinking again. He had a considerable investment portfolio and enough capital to pull it off. He had the corporate business savvy to stay employed with Manning for nearly ten years. And he certainly had the background and love of cooking to carry him through the running of a restaurant. But did he really know anything about managing a business like that? It was one thing to cook for a few people, friends and family. Dealing personally with hundreds of customers every night was a different matter altogether. The logistics of anticipating and ordering sufficient amounts of food and–

His phone rang again, and he picked it up immediately, dropping the idea of owning and running his own restaurant. It was just a pipedream anyway ... not something he could seriously consider.

He recognized the voice on the line and quickly assumed his most professional stance. This, he suspected, was his curtain call. He'd either be reassigned or...

* * * * *

"So, have you talked to Cole yet?" Chelle prodded.

Seated on Chelle's pristine white couch, Kari shook her head and looked away.

"Why not? It's obvious you two are gaga over each other."

Kari shrugged, helpless to offer a realistic explanation. She'd avoided Cole at first because she was hurt and angry over the fact that he'd lied to her. But after the days had passed, and he hadn't made further attempts to contact her beyond the initial phone calls, she convinced herself that he wasn't that interested in apologizing and making amends. Anyway, it wasn't like they'd actually been dating or anything. He'd just cooked her dinner a couple times, and let her cat make himself at home in his apartment.

She blinked in astonishment, realizing finally how personal those seemingly simple overtures were. What man went to the trouble of cooking dinner multiple times for a woman he barely knew? What man allowed a strange cat into his apartment and went to the trouble of making the animal feel at home? *A very special man – a man who had the capacity to genuinely care.*

"I've been an idiot, haven't I?" Kari said suddenly, shooting up from Chelle's couch.

"Well, yeah. Sort of."

"I mean, he tried to apologize, tried to explain, but I wouldn't even give him a chance."

Chelle rose from her chair slowly and eyed Kari. "So ... does this mean you've had a change of heart?"

Kari shrugged and then turned away, shaking her head. "I-I don't know what to do. I can't call him now, after–"

"Sure you can. I bet he's just been waiting for you to come around."

Smiling, Kari sighed and turned to face Chelle. "I'll call him tomorrow."

"Why wait? Call him now."

Kari glanced at her watch. She'd had dinner with Chelle, and they'd come back to her apartment for coffee and a late-night chat. It was nearly 10:00, and Chelle had to go to work tomorrow. So did Cole. "I don't want to wake him."

Chelle picked up her coffee cup and took a sip. "Suit yourself. But if I were you, I wouldn't waste any time if I really cared about the guy."

Smirking, Kari nodded. "I gotta go. I'll talk to you later." She darted forward and hugged Chelle. "Thanks."

"No problem. Go get 'im, girl."

The Cat's Fancy Gwynn E. Ambrose

Kari laughed as she headed out of Chelle's condo to her car parked in the underground garage. With keys in hand, she dug her cell phone out of her handbag and dialed the number saved in her 'missed calls' log.

As she rode the elevator down to the basement, the number rang several times, then went to voicemail. Frowning, Kari hung up without leaving a message. She was caught off guard, realizing she hadn't prepared what to say to Cole, and she felt a message would just make her sound whiny and desperate. She needed to talk to Cole in person, face-to-face. She'd wait until tomorrow afternoon when he came home from work to go over to his apartment and grovel for a second chance.

* * * * *

When Kari got back to her apartment, it was after eleven, but Max was up waiting for her, eager to go out the patio doors.

"Baby, it's too late for you to go out tonight," she said, putting her keys and purse down on the coffee table.

Max meowed, insistent, as he stood before the patio doors and batted at the closed vertical blinds.

"All right," Kari capitulated, walking over to unlock the doors and slide them open. "But you can only go out for a few minutes. I want you back in here when I call. You got it?"

Max purred a 'whatever' meow and slipped outside into the darkness.

* * * * *

Cole was still up, packing the last of his meager personal belongings, when he heard the rattle and meow on his balcony. Surprised, he went over to the patio doors and opened them to look out. Max came trotting in like he owned the place.

"Hey, buddy. Long time no see," Cole said as Max made the rounds, investigating the boxes sitting around in the living room. Max turned and looked at him, letting out a peculiar tonal meow, as if he were questioning what was going on.

"Time to go, my furry friend. I'm heading back to stay with my folks in St. Louis for a while. The Hatchet Man's out of a job."

Max meowed again, this time with a seeming plaintive note. Cole smiled wistfully. "Yeah, I feel the same way. That's the thanks I get for ten years of unwavering service. But at least I'm getting a hefty severance package."

Max looked at him, then went over and poked his nose in a box, sniffing at the items inside. When he seemed satisfied with his identification and assessment of the contents, he strolled over and jumped up on the couch.

"Don't get too comfortable there, Max. It's late, and you're definitely not spending the night here. Anyway, I've arranged with the apartment manager to see that your favorite couch goes back to the rental place tomorrow morning."

Max meowed, seeming disgruntled, then settled in, as if he were preparing for a night-long snooze.

"You better get on back home," Cole warned. "I'm leaving bright and early in the morning, and I won't have time to herd you back to where you belong. Besides, I don't think your owner wants to see me. So let's say our goodbyes now, shall we?"

Cole headed for the couch to shoo Max toward the patio doors, but Max never budged as he approached. Cole stood over him, thinking for a second that the cat was again presenting him with the perfect opportunity to weasel his way back into Kari's good graces, but he nixed that idea immediately. He was out of a job and had no reason to stay another day in Baltimore – especially when Kari had made it clear she wanted nothing more to do with him.

He shook his head and bent down, gently scooping up the cat in his arms. "Come on, big boy. Time to go home."

Max seemed a little disgruntled as Cole plopped him down on the carpet in front of the patio doors. "Go on, now. Go home,

Max." Cole pointed and used his foot to guide Max out through the doors.

Complaining with another disgruntled yowl, Max slipped out the patio doors. Cole reached to close the doors, then heard the timer go off on the microwave. He turned and went into the kitchen to fetch his late-night snack, forgetting about the partially open patio doors...

CHAPTER 14

Max the Matchmaker's Machinations

Kari was still up at midnight waiting for Max to come home. She'd called and called for him, hoping she wasn't disturbing her neighbors, but he never showed. Figuring he'd come in when he was good and ready – typical cat – she finally went to bed, leaving the patio doors open for his eventual return.

* * * * *

I sat in the darkness, watching Cole's open patio doors, wondering what he'd do if I darted back inside his apartment. The loud beep from the kitchen, signaling food, snagged Cole's attention before he closed his glass doors. Now they stood open, inviting me back in. I licked a paw and washed my face, thinking about it.

I could hear the faint, far-off sound of Kari's voice calling for me, but I kept my vigil outside Cole's abode, planning my next move. Eventually Kari's calls ceased, as I assumed they would when she went off to bed.

Somehow I had to get Cole to come to Kari's domicile. I thought sitting down on the couch would force him to take me home, but he had simply urged me back out the doors through which I'd come – and he hadn't bothered to offer me a tasty snack as he usually did. This, plus the sight of boxes filled with various items, unsettled me. When I'd first noticed Cole in this apartment, I had seen boxes sitting around, some empty and some partially filled with items similar to those I'd noticed when he'd

The Cat's Fancy GWYNN E. Ambrose

first moved in. Now the boxes were back, making me think that Cole was on the move again. This definitely did not fit with my plans.

Why did humans have to be so difficult? Kari had been lonely enough to accept the company of male humans totally unsuitable for her, and yet when I'd found her a perfectly suitable mate – one who could prepare delicious food for my personal enjoyment – she resisted my matchmaking efforts by staying away from Cole after she'd clearly begun to like him. Cole seemed to like her as well, yet he did not pursue her. What else was needed for them to see that they belonged together, not only for their mutual well-being, but for mine as well?

I thought back to our last evening together, when everything seemed to go wrong. Something had happened to disturb everyone's happiness when Raschelle had come over. Something had upset Kari when she took me back to the apartment that night. I didn't know what that something was, but I was determined not to let it sway my plan for Kari and Cole. Somehow ... somehow I had to convince Cole and Kari to mend their differences, because the two of them belonged together – and I deserved all the benefits of their happiness.

I noticed Cole closing and fastening the last of his boxes in the living room. After he completed this task and stacked the boxes by the door, he turned off the lights and headed toward his bedroom, obviously forgetting he'd left his patio doors open. I moved forward, toward the still parted patio doors. It was my job to investigate the situation and find a suitable solution, and of course I was ready to meet that challenge.

* * * * *

In the parking lot below the apartment he'd just vacated, Cole loaded the last of the boxes and packed them in the tiny space left in the trailer hitched to his car. He checked the hitch once more to make sure everything was well secured and the safety chains wouldn't drag the ground. And then he went to his car and activated the turn signal for first the left and then the right blinkers to make sure the lights on the trailer were working properly.

Satisfied, he went back to his car and rested a hand on the open driver's door. Standing outside the car, he checked his watch – right on schedule at 7:30 – and then looked up at the second floor, to apartment 2B. Kari's apartment.

He noticed the heavy vines cloaking the balcony supports, figuring that was how Kari's cat got down to the ground floor for his outdoor forays. Max was apparently quite a skilled climber to scale the vertical column of vines – up and down – and not fall.

Fantasizing, Cole imaged spotting Kari on the balcony, beckoning to him at the last minute to wait until she could come down and talk him out of leaving. But he saw neither Kari nor her black cat. Sighing, he accepted reality and slid into the driver's seat of his car.

Pulling the door shut, he started the car, but before he backed out, he decided to try one more time to talk to Kari. He grabbed his cell phone and dialed her apartment number. It rang and rang. Before it could go to voicemail, he hung up and set his phone aside. It was time to get on the road. He had a long drive to St. Louis, and he wanted to pick up breakfast at a drive-up to save time. He'd promised his mother he'd be there by dinnertime that evening.

* * * * *

Kari awoke with a start, realizing the phone was ringing for real, not just in her dream. On impulse she picked up the receiver and answered with a groggy, "Hello?" but was met with a dial tone. Whoever had called had hung up an instant before she picked up. Annoyed and unsettled, she flopped back down on the bed. Then it dawned on her that Max was not sleeping comfortably at her feet.

The Cat's Fancy

Gwynn E. Ambrose

She propped herself up in the bed and looked around. "Max? Maxi? Where are you, baby?"

She'd let him out late last night, and if he'd come back in after she'd gone to bed, he'd gone out again before she had woken up. With a vague feeling of uneasiness, she got out of bed and went to the bathroom. "He'll show up when he's good and ready," she reassured herself.

* * * * *

By 9:30, Kari found herself in a state of emotional desperation. She'd called repeatedly for Max, inside and outside, and had heard no response. It wasn't like him to take off and stay gone for hours and hours. By this time, she feared something had happened to him. Panic gripped her, and she fought back tears as she tried not to imagine all the menacing situations that could have befallen her cat.

Luckily, about that time Chelle called, temporarily relieving Kari of the worries about her cat. "What's up, Chelle?" Kari asked listlessly.

"Have you talked to Cole yet?" Chelle prodded.

"No. I called but his cell last night, but it was late, and he didn't answer. I was going to wait until he came home from work this afternoon to talk to him in person. Why?"

"Well, you might be a little late. Lori told me this morning she'd heard Cole was let go from Manning Friday afternoon. He hasn't showed up for work, so I'm guessing the rumors are true."

"Let go? You mean...?"

"Fired. Guess they didn't need his Hatchet Man services anymore."

Kari slumped down in a kitchen chair, stunned by the news. "How could they do that?"

"Same way they got rid of you. They don't care about anybody. It's just business to them. They're looking at the bottom line, and any way they can improve that, they're going to go for it, no matter what it means to employees. Guess Cole's number was up."

"Oh my." Kari felt bad for him. She knew what it was like to have the rug pulled out from under her. "What's he going to do now?"

"I imagine he's going to pack up and leave – if he hasn't already," Chelle said ominously.

Kari felt her heart seize at the thought. "But ... but I–"

"Yeah, you fooled around and let him slip through your fingers. You'd better call him right now and find out what's going on."

As Kari ended her call with Chelle, she gripped the phone and paced into her living room, wondering now not only about what had happened to Max, but what Cole was going to do. Surely he was preparing to pack up and leave at this very moment. With her cat missing, Kari couldn't think straight, and the news about Cole made it even more difficult for her to concentrate.

When she thought about Cole, her panic level went even higher. She'd lost her opportunity to be with a perfectly wonderful man, just because of a little problem of him lying about who he was and who he worked for. But that didn't matter now. He didn't work for Manning Industries anymore, and if Chelle was right, he was in the process of leaving Baltimore – before she could tell him how she felt about him. She didn't know if her feelings would make any difference to him at this point, but she owed it to herself to at least let him know. Where he would be going, she had no idea, but she had to head him off before he left so she could talk to him. She grabbed her cell phone to find his cell number still stored in her missed calls log.

* * * * *

Cole had been on the road for nearly an hour and a half, finally reaching Interstate 70. He'd chowed down on his egg and cheese and bacon biscuit with coffee and orange juice, and was just settling into the flow of traffic when an unexpected noise grabbed his attention – the faint meow of a cat.

"Wha–" Cole quickly glanced over his shoulder and saw a black cat – Max – emerge from the bundles of hanging clothes lying in the tight quarters of the back-seat area. "How in the world did you...?"

Max meowed louder and crawled over the console to situate himself in the passenger seat beside Cole. "Oh boy..." Cole said. "We've got a problem."

Before he could even think of calling Kari to let her know her mischievous cat had stowed away in his car, his cell phone rang. "Kari," he answered, somewhat surprised.

"Cole, I know I've been avoiding you for the last week, but–"

"Kari, before you say anything else, I want to apologize for–"

"I don't care about that now. I just wanted to tell you I'd heard that you'd lost your job, and–"

"News travels fast. Especially bad news – or good news, depending on who's telling it."

"Well, ... I need to talk to you, and I was wondering if I could come over to your place and–"

"That's going to be a little difficult, since it's not technically my place anymore."

"Wh-What do you mean?"

"I turned in my keys and checked out this morning," Cole said. "The rental company's supposed to pick up the furniture sometime today. I'm on the road, headed for St. Louis right now. And before you say anything else, I have to tell you something."

Kari paused, then asked in a low tone, "What?"

"I have your cat."

"What! You ... you stole Max?"

"No, I didn't steal him. I didn't take him on purpose. I mean, I didn't take him at all. I didn't know he'd hopped in my car while I was packing up this morning. And I took off, and he was ... in here, in the car with me. He just now came out from hiding."

"Oh my gosh!" Kari gushed. "I was so worried about him! I thought something had happened..."

Cole could hear her voice cracking, as if she were on the verge of tears. "It's okay, Kari. I'm turning off the interstate at the next exit. I'll get him back to you as soon as I can."

"I-I'm sorry, Cole, to make you have to double back and..."

He heard her gulp, and then there was silence. "It's okay, Kari. I want to make sure I get him back to you. I know how much he means to you."

He heard a couple sobs, then she gulped again and said quickly, in a high-pitched tone, "Thanks, Cole. I ... I'm sorry about your job. I wish I'd ... I'll talk to you when you get back."

"I'll call you on your cell when I get back into Baltimore."

"Yeah, okay," she squeaked. She ended the call, and Cole set his phone aside, curious about her heightened emotional state. She seemed to be upset about more than just her missing cat.

* * * * *

Kari was waiting out on the balcony with her cell phone in hand when Cole called again to let her know he was pulling into the Garden Plaza parking lot. She ran back into her apartment and shot out the front door to race down the steps and meet him as he emerged from his car with Max in his arms.

"Oh, Maxi, you bad, bad kitty! Mommy was so worried about you!" She scooped him out of Cole's arms and hugged him tight. "You are very naughty! Bad kitty! And you made Cole drive all the way back here..."

Max squirmed in her arms, and she let him down on the pavement. Looking up at Cole, she offered an apologetic smile. "I'm really sorry you had to double back and–"

"I'm not," he said decisively, moving close to stand in front

The Cat's Fancy

of her. "I didn't want to leave without saying goodbye – properly." Before she could react to that statement, he took her face in his hands and planted a soft, exploring kiss on her lips. When he pulled back finally to look her in the eyes, all she could do was gasp in surprise.

"I'm sorry I lied to you, Kari," he said, still holding her face in his hands. "It was a spur of the moment thing. I was surprised to find myself living down the hall from you, knowing you'd worked at Manning, and I was sort of in the opposite camp. I didn't think things through before I did it, and then afterward I realized what an awkward mistake I'd made. I never intended to try and pull anything over on you. All I wanted was to make sure you–"

"I know," she squawked with tears streaming down her face just as she finally regained the ability to speak. "I was stupid and stubborn not to let you at least explain. And when I finally thought things through, I realized–"

He cut her off by kissing her again. She let herself melt against him as she circled her arms around him. When he parted his lips from hers and rested his chin on her head, she whispered, "This doesn't feel like 'goodbye.'"

"It doesn't, does it?" He chuckled and added, "of course, if I stay, I'm going to be without a place to crash."

She pulled back to face him, grinning sheepishly as she offered, "I've got a very uncomfortable red couch you can use temporarily."

He snapped his fingers. "Or I can get back the couch that Max loves ... but where would we put it?"

Kari lit up with a wild idea. "I think I know the perfect place!"

CHAPTER 15

Epilogue – Max's Place

Raschelle watched with satisfaction as the small but efficient construction crew finished installing the industrial lighting suspended from the dark, open-beam ceiling. Of particular interest was Derek, the very fine owner of the construction and renovation company. He worked right alongside his crew and was not afraid to get his hands dirty. *But my, my, he cleans up well!*

Tall, muscular, decisive, and extremely friendly toward her, he made it a point to consult her on every detail of the old building's refurbishment, even though technically she was not the owner, just the manager of the restaurant that would soon open in the renovated space. When she had revealed to Cole that she and her ex had owned and managed a profitable nightclub in New York City, he was able to offer her the management job he'd hinted at when he was still at Manning Industries. That management job at Manning, of course, did not materialize once his time at Manning was cut short. But what he offered her instead was much more appealing.

Managing his restaurant was like a dream recaptured. When she and her ex-louse Devon had owned and operated the nightclub RD's, she had loved the whole atmosphere and bustle of people coming and going. The social aspects of dealing with restaurant customers would not be the same, but it appealed immensely to her for that very reason. People would be coming in to enjoy the food and the atmosphere, not to 'hook up' or get buzzed. People would appreciate the effort she and the staff of the restaurant would put in every day to make their visit enjoyable and memorable. And with Cole's recipes at the heart of everything, it was a winning situation for everyone. She didn't regret for a moment leaving her call-center job at Manning. She knew her future belonged here, with her friends Kari and Cole.

The job at Manning had been a temporary diversion at best, something she'd taken on the spur of the moment when she fled New York after the dust had settled from her divorce. She'd hated giving up the nightclub, but Devon had siphoned off so much money from it, she'd been lucky to pay off what she and he had owed on the place and its outstanding operating expenses. Luckily for her, she'd kept her personal finances separate so that Devon couldn't tap those funds too. The financial cushion allowed her to relocate with style and accept a job that didn't pay anything close to what she knew she was worth. And she hadn't planned on staying at Manning nearly as long as she had.

But now things were looking up, and she was anticipating with excitement the opening of the restaurant. The only trouble was, Cole and Kari couldn't decide on a name for it, and therefore hadn't ordered signage for the outside of the building, or menus, or – oh, there was so much more to do, and so little time before the scheduled opening.

Her professional worries melted when Derek turned on his ladder and looked down at her with another gleaming smile. His chocolate skin glowed like he was an angel anointed on high. And despite the fact that his name was similar to her ex Devon's – she could overlook that unfortunate similarity because he was nothing like Devon – she allowed herself the secret luxury of fantasizing about a future with him. It had been a long time since she'd seriously eyed a handsome black man with the idea of a long-term relationship. She could tell he was a man capable of caring and loving, and that's what she wanted and needed, she'd discovered suddenly. With the recent changes in her life, it seemed like the perfect time ... especially since Kari and Cole were going to tie the knot soon.

She smiled back at Derek, winking at him to signal that tonight ... tonight she'd let him know how serious she really was. His smile widened in response.

* * * * *

Kari walked through the restaurant with Cole to survey the progress on the building. She was amazed how the renovations so far had changed the character of the interior – especially the upstairs living area they'd turned into a spacious apartment for themselves, and of course for Max. Max seemed to revel in his new domain, especially when he realized the back stairway allowed him to go downstairs and outside to a private garden area behind the building, comfortably shaded with mature trees.

The main level, the site of Cole's restaurant and her gallery attached to one side had undergone an amazing transformation. The building interior was no longer a dusty, sad repository of old shelving, discarded two-by-fours, and miscellaneous junk, most of which was trash. The raw brick walls had been scrubbed, giving the rustic interior a quaint feel offset by the high ceiling painted black to match the suspension beams installed for the industrial track lighting and pendant lighting that cast diffused light everywhere for a cozy yet eclectic evening atmosphere. During the day, the tall arched windows let in an abundance of light that was tempered with wooden shutters. The very top of the arched portion of the windows had been left uncovered for a clearstory effect. Overall, the space was awesome, with its meandering alcoves created by previous architectural modifications Derek, their contractor, was able to seamlessly blend in for a unified look.

"What do you think, Chef Cole?" Kari asked, looking up to find Cole admiring the work as keenly as she was.

"It's coming along. Once we move in the extra furniture for the lounge areas, and hang all your pictures up on the walls to create different artistic treatments in each area, I think it'll be stunning and eye-catching."

Kari scrunched up her nose. "You're not seriously going to hang all those pictures up that I painted of Max. They're kind of slap-dash. I was in a funk mood when I painted them."

Cole grinned. "A bad mood because I wasn't around at the time to cook dinner for you every night."

Kari rolled her eyes, ignoring the fact that it had been her decision to avoid Cole after she learned of his affiliation with Manning.

"Anyway, I think those pictures are really good. They're all different, but they each somehow manage to catch some essence of Max – his feline superiority, his aloofness, his royal laziness. You did a great job portraying him in each one, making the compositions not just run-of-the-mill pictures of cats, but real works of art that catch the eye and hold the viewer's attention."

"You should be an art critic. You sound like you know more about painting than I do."

He touched a finger to her nose in playful admonishment. "Stop devaluing what you're naturally good at. Who knows ... maybe someone will want to buy a few of your paintings, if you'd let people see them. If you're not going to hang them in your own gallery next door, at least let me use them to decorate the restaurant."

"Then what? We'll call the place *The Cat House?*" Kari teased.

Cole laughed, then stopped and assumed a serious look. "Well, why not? We have to come up with some name for the restaurant soon. Otherwise Chelle's going to shoot me and call it *Chelle's Diner*. We don't have signs or menus or–"

"Cole, we can't call it The Cat House! Both your parents and mine would have a fit. We'd probably offend half our potential customers. Your mom and dad would refuse to move here to help us out, and your mom would never step foot in the kitchen, leaving you doing all the cooking and kitchen supervising yourself every night. And I'd never see you!"

"Well, we can't have that!" He ducked down and stole a kiss from her, and she playfully slapped at him. He stuck a finger to his chin, exaggerating yet another great idea suddenly realized. "Well, since we'll have all your cat paintings gracing the walls, and we'll be decorating with eclectic furniture to match the styles of the various paintings in each of the individual dining areas—"

"Which I still think is a terrible idea."

"Trust me. Didn't you tell me the first time we met that you should take decorating tips from me?"

Kari laughed, remembering entering Cole's apartment to fetch her wayward cat, and thinking how serene and inviting his apartment looked in comparison to the hard colors and chaotic patterns she'd chosen to decorate her own place down the hall. "Yes, you're right."

"Of course I am. And really, it was Max who brought us together in the first place, and brought us back together when I left after my job at Manning ended. So it's only fitting we should hang some pictures of Max around the place, and maybe even..."

"...name the place after Max too?"

He shrugged. "*Max's Place*. Sounds to me like the perfect name for a restaurant. Don't you think so?"

Kari frowned, thinking about it, then felt her face bloom with a smile. Of course. It *was* perfect. "And I could call my gallery area—"

"The Cat House!" Cole suggested exuberantly.

"No!" Kari punched him in the arm, then looked away to think seriously about it. She felt the idea forming in her mind like a cloud of mist coalescing into a real idea. "The ... The Cat . . The Cat's Fancy!" She turned and looked up at Cole. "What do you think?"

Cole bowed his head and kissed her. "Great! Now we can order the signs and menus, and Chelle will get off my case."

* * * * *

131

The Cat's Fancy

Gwynn E. Ambrose

As I sat on my second favorite couch in the whole place – my first choice being the cushy one I originally discovered in Cole's apartment, which was now in our living room upstairs – I surveyed my new and changing surroundings, unsettled yet pleased by the renovation progress made on the building Kari and Cole recently acquired. The furniture was all in place, offering me many choices for lounging.

Although I'd overheard Kari and Cole discussing with Raschelle the health regulations regarding my presence downstairs in a place where they planned to serve food daily to a customer base that was exclusively human, the ramifications of this development – soon to happen, if the progress of redecorating was any indication – did not concern me. With free run of the living area upstairs, I could go outside to the garden level at any time of my choosing, with plenty of native creatures to entertain me. I was sure my humans would thank me later for eradicating the infestation of mice I discovered near the building foundation – once they saw the evidence I'd left in plain sight for them to find.

Raschelle had spent almost every day here, seeming to have made peace with me and no longer referring to me as 'that evil cat.' Once in a while she even rubbed me behind the ears. Of course I always purred for her, as it would be bad form to alienate a human that Kari was very fond of and who now spent almost as much time here as Cole and Kari did. Raschelle seemed to exert as much dominion over the area downstairs as Kari and Cole, so I decided to give her wide berth. She'd also been showing inordinate interest in the man making changes to the building, and so I expected to see him here more often, even after his work here was completed.

Kari seemed quite pleased with our new situation. She and Cole shared the largest bedroom at the end of the apartment upstairs, and Kari had brought home many magazines featuring photos of young women dressed in voluminous dresses with veils. She seemed preoccupied with these magazines, intent on making plans for some event early in the fall, to take place in the gallery area, with a reception to follow in the restaurant downstairs.

Her smaller portion of the building on one side, with its separate front entrance and small eating area, had been set up to serve as the local art gallery she apparently has always dreamed of owning. Not only did she plan to feature the work of area artists, but she'd also made arrangements with the nearby art school to showcase student work for sale. She planned to draw customers in by serving daily 'lunch at the gallery' from 11:00 to 2:00, featuring Cole's culinary specialties. The gallery's dining space would make money from the lunch crowd while offering passive opportunities for art sales. The gallery luncheon menu would be completely different from Cole's main restaurant menu, catering to the tastes of the rich elite socialite set that presumably harbored a native interest in collecting and displaying original art.

Apparently, since I was somehow responsible for all this – Cole and Kari's relationship and their joint restaurant-gallery endeavor – they named both the restaurant and the gallery after me, or at least in my honor. Of course I admit I have little real experience with human cuisine or artistic expression. I only enjoy eating some select human foods, and the only cooking I've done was hopping up on the counter and knocking a wok of frozen stir-fry onto a hot stove burner. The smell was horrendous – burnt broccoli is offensive, to say the least. The only painting I've ever done was tracking paint from Kari's palette onto the carpet, and the only way I held a paint brush was by chewing on it. Those methods of creative expressions definitely didn't impress Kari.

Considering everything, I figured I was the very first cat in feline history to be a matchmaker for human relationships, owner of a human restaurant and art gallery, and celebrated cat model and budding artist. Over all, I'd say I did pretty well for everyone involved. *Fancy that!*

~About the Author~

GWYNN E. AMBROSE is an animal lover and enjoys injecting the crazy fun of animals into her stories. She advocates animal rights and fair and decent treatment of animals. Gwynn also is an artist and enjoys painting and drawing all kinds of subjects, including animals. She dabbles in web pages and electronic art, and has created several book covers, including the one for this book. *The Cat's Fancy* is Gwynn's first novel. To find out more about Gwynn, please visit her web site at...

http://www.gwynneambrose.com